An Augat

ANNIE SEATON

Augathella Short and Sweet: 4

Annie Seaton

Copyright © 2023 Annie Seaton

All rights reserved.

ISBN 9781923048225

AUGATHELLA SHORT AND SWEETS

An Augathella Surprise

An Augathella Baby

An Augathella Spring

An Augathella Christmas

An Augathella Wedding

An Augathella Winter

An Augathella Ball

Following on from:

THE AUGATHELLA GIRLS

Book 1: Outback Roads –The Nanny

Book 2: Outback Sky – The Pilot

Book 3: Outback Escape – The Sister

Book 4: Outback Winds – The Jillaroo

Book 5: Outback Dawn – The Visitor

Book 6: Outback Moonlight – The Rogue

Book 7: Outback Dust – The Drifter

Book 8: Outback Hope – The Farmer

Annie Seaton

CHAPTER 1

Sophie

Sophie Mason leaned back in the swivel chair that had been delivered a few days before Ruby Rose was born. A pale dove-grey colour matched the doona cover and the two plump red cushions made the soft chair perfect for breastfeeding. Its position—tucked into the corner of their bedroom between the two picture windows—provided a pretty outlook over their front house paddock. Sophie had continued Kent's mother's gardening when his parents had moved to Brisbane, and the front garden was full of early summer blooms. During Ruby's night feeds, Sophie sat with a dim nightlight beside her and looked out at the star-studded outback sky.

She smiled when she saw Kent loading the baby bags she'd packed earlier for him to put into the back of her SUV.

The gentle movement against her breast made Sophie look down. Even though it was two weeks since their little girl had been born, Sophie's heart still flooded with emotion each time she looked at her baby's face. A contented sigh escaped Ruby Rose's mouth as her lips slipped off Sophie's breast and her little rosy cheek rested against Sophie's skin. She was a perfect baby and had fed like a charm from the first hour of her life.

Callie shook her head the first time she came to visit.

'She's been feeding for six minutes,' Sophie said as she supported Ruby on her lap with her fingers beneath her chin and rubbed her back gently. 'She'll stay asleep now.'

'My God, Sophie, do you know how lucky you are?' Callie reached down and ran her fingers lightly down Ruby's cheek. 'The first week Munro and Megan were born, they were taking over an hour for each feed. An hour each! Two hours of feeding and then they were awake in another three hours and it all started again. I don't know what I would have done without Braden there helping with the double nappy changes, and the burping!'

'Our Ruby Rose is a champion.'

Sophie smiled when Kent, the proudest dad in the world, chimed in. 'She knows what she wants, and she goes for it, and fills her little tummy in a couple of minutes.'

Sophie swapped Ruby to the other breast to see if she wanted more, but her eyes stayed tightly shut and her lips pursed. If she stuck to her normal routine, it would be five hours before she woke with a soft little cry, had a quick feed and then went back to sleep.

Sophie had worried at first that there was something wrong with her newborn because of all the horror stories she'd heard about feeding.

Laura Adnum, the midwife who delivered her had been satisfied with Ruby's progress when Sophie and Kent had gone into town last week.

'She's gained half a kilogram, Sophie.'

'Is that enough?'

'That's perfect and shows that she's feeding beautifully.' Laura said. 'Now, how are you?'

'I'm remarkably relaxed and getting good sleep every night,' Sophie said. 'It's so much easier than I expected!'

'Keep it up.' Laura smiled as she handed Ruby back to Sophie. 'We'll see you here after Christmas for your six-week check-up.'

Now Sophie leaned back into her chair and ran her finger over Ruby's fine blonde hair. Her lips were pursed in a beautiful rosebud; she and Kent had come up with the middle name of Rose even before they had noticed her little rosebud lips.

Rose had been Braden and Sophie's

grandmother's name, and Sophie wanted to have that connection to the Cartwright side.

'How long before you're ready?' Kent appeared in the doorway. 'Looks like she's finished feeding.'

Sophie looked up. 'I'll get ready now if you can take her. She can go in the car carrier as soon as I get changed. Won't take me long.'

'The car's packed.'

'Yes, I saw you loading it while she fed.'

Sophie buttoned up her shirt, and then placed Ruby on her shoulder, giving her a little pat. A soft belch came from Ruby's lips, and her head flopped down on Sophie's shoulder.

'She's sound asleep already.' Sophie smiled up at Kent.

'I'm happy to hold her while you get ready,' he said with a wide grin. 'Take your time.' Kent hovered beside the chair, and Sophie smiled up at her husband.

'Okay, I'll get ready. I had my shower when I got up this morning when you were out in the shed.'

'Come to Daddy, beautiful girl.' Kent took Ruby Rose from Sophie and pressed his lips against her forehead.

Sophie stood. 'I think we have a little girl who is going to be spoiled rotten by her daddy.'

Kent's smile said it all. 'We're staying at Kilcoy for dinner, aren't we?' he asked as he settled in the chair.

'Sorry, didn't I tell you? Yes, Callie said we'll have an early barbie. It'll be good to catch up with them all.' Sophie glanced back from the door before she walked into the hallway. The look of love on Kent's face as he looked down at Ruby Rose brought another tear to her eye. It was the only after-effect of pregnancy and childbirth she was having. She was always so damn emotional, but with a husband like Kent and a perfect baby, she had a good reason to be.

CHAPTER 2

Callie

'So, what date can we go to the Gold Coast?' Braden reached in and took out the tray of meat from the bottom shelf.

Callie lifted Munro to her shoulder and patted his back.

Braden smiled when a satisfying burp emitted from the three-month-old's lips. 'That's my boy,' he said. Callie handed Munro to Braden and reached for Meg who was in the double pram beside the table.

'Your dad still doesn't know how to burp you, does he, sweetheart?'

Callie smiled and looked at her husband as a delicate puff of wind came from between Meg's lips. 'That's my girl.'

'Do you think I've got enough meat out of the freezer?' Braden asked as he held Munro with one hand, and with the other put the tray of almost defrosted meat on the sink tray.

'Give me a couple of minutes. I'll just put them in the cot, and we'll talk about dates,' she said. 'And yes, that's heaps of steak.' She reached over and took Munro from Braden and nursed him as she pushed the pram up the hall to the nursery.

The three boys were playing outside, and Callie could hear them giggling as she walked up the hallway. The twins both went down very quickly, and she stood there for a moment, looking at their plump cheeks as they drifted off in the cot beside each other.

When she walked back down the hall to the kitchen, Braden had made a fresh pot of tea, and she sat beside him at the table.

'What on earth are those boys doing?' she asked. They were still giggling, and occasionally, there was a happy scream followed by loud laughter.

Braden shook his head. 'I don't know. I was going to go and have a listen because Nigel's almost hysterical with laughter. Something's amused them.'

Callie put her hand on his arm. 'It's good to see, isn't it? Nigel's been so good these last few months.'

'Especially since the twins arrived. He seems to have grown up a little bit,' Braden said. 'And he's so much happier.'

They both looked at each other and smiled as another shriek of laughter drifted up the back steps.

'What *are* they doing?' Braden poured Callie's tea and added two spoons of sugar to his black tea. He got up and walked across to the back door and looked outside.

Callie watched her husband as he stood there. Braden said that Nigel had been happy, but since the twins had been born there had been a shift in him too. He had been happy enough when she first met him, but now that they were married and had Megan and Munro, as well as Petie, Nigel, and Rory, who she considered as hers now, Braden had shed the worry and angst that had sometimes dogged him. These days he was always smiling and whistling, his shoulders were straight, and he didn't even worry about the property as much now. Fair enough, the rains had been good through the winter, and they had nothing to worry about financially, but even though that had been the case before, he had always managed to find a problem when there was none.

Now a grin spread across his lips as he tipped his head to the side. He listened to the boys for a while longer, then shook his head as he walked back across the kitchen.

Callie held her hand up and caught Braden's

hand as he moved past her to sit down.

'I love you, Braden Cartwright.'

He paused before leaning down and brushing his lips over hers.

'And I love you too, Mrs Cartwright.' His eyes held hers as he sat down and he picked up his mug. 'What brought that on? Not that I'm complaining.'

Callie smiled. 'Nothing special. I'm just happy. And I'm very content.'

'So am I.' Braden grinned. 'Even if our sleep is being interrupted every night.'

Another scream and more laughter came inside.

'What are they doing?' she asked curiously.

'I believe from what I overheard that they are writing a play.'

'A play?' Callie's eyes opened wide. 'Ah, I know what they're doing. Kimberley's got a contest running at school as part of the literacy program.'

'A contest?'

'Yes. She's invited all the students from Prep to year six; if they write a play for the Christmas concert in the last week of school, one play will be chosen to be performed by some of the children.'

'And it sounds like the boys are right into it.' Braden chuckled. 'Although I don't know if what I heard would be suitable for a school audience.'

'Oh dear. I hope no swearing?'

'No. But I'm sure they'll tell you about it. I won't spoil the surprise. You can judge for yourself.'

'Okay, Kimberley has given them some great motivation. Whoever writes the winning play, will be able to choose the cast.'

'So, it's supposed to be a nativity play?' Braden asked.

'Well, sort of. All they have to do is have Joseph and Mary and baby Jesus in it, and they can do what they want with the story. It doesn't even have to be in the stable. They don't have to have the three wise men. They just have to write a story, an original story that teaches of the joy of Christmas.'

Braden laughed. 'Does there have to be a donkey in it?'

'A donkey? Why?'

'Yes, there's always a donkey at the manger. I think the boys have picked that up.'

Callie frowned. 'From memory, I think Kimberley did give them some examples and she did tell them that some nativity plays have been written from the donkey's point of view. Is that what they're doing?'

Braden's eyes gleamed with mirth. 'Not exactly, but you'll see.'

'Tell me, Braden. Do I need to censor it

before they hand it in?'

'Um, how about a farting donkey at the manger? I heard some of the sound effects from Nigel when Petie screamed before.'

'Oh, my goodness, maybe I'd better read it!'

'No, let them go. They're boys and they're having fun, and working together without fighting! Besides, we could be away for the concert. Now, what day have we got all the Christmas stuff over and done with?'

'Well, we've got the school dinner at the pub on the ninth, and then we've got dinner with all our friends the next night. I've got an afternoon tea at Jenna's tea room on the fourteenth—the last day of school. And then we're free.'

Braden rolled his eyes. 'That's going to be a big weekend with two nights out.'

'Yes, it is, but I've already lined Ruth up. She's happy to have the twins. We can take the kids to the Sunday night family one, but Ruth's happy to have the boys on the Saturday night as well as the twins.'

'Isn't that a bit much to ask?' Braden asked. 'Looking after the *five* of them?'

'Ruth said Fallon and Jon will be there and they'll help out. Apparently, she's minding Emily's Ophelia too.'

'We're so lucky to have Ruth in town, aren't we?' he said. 'I wouldn't have asked Sophie. Not for a while anyway.'

'We are, and no. Sophie is busy with Ruby Rose. Okay, so we're clear from the sixteenth of December, the end of the last week of term.'

'Good. That works out well. If I book the apartment from the nineteenth, it gives us time to get down there for four days and still be home for Christmas Day. How does that sound? We'll have to leave on the Saturday morning after your do at the tea room.'

'Yeah, that sounds okay,' Callie said slowly.

'But?' Braden said. He knew her well, Callie thought.

'The only problem is that Saturday is the day the play will be on at the school hall. The boys would probably want to be there.'

'I don't think a farting donkey story will be chosen though, do you?'

'Probably not.'

'Okay, that's the date sorted. I'll book the unit online after Sophie and Kent leave after dinner. I've already put a hold on it for that week. I just have to pay the deposit.'

'I guess Sea World, Dream World, and Movie World will sweeten missing the concert for them, plus we'll be home for Santa Claus presents on Christmas Day.'

'Saves lugging the presents to the coast.' Braden nodded. 'The boys will be fine. We'll have to tell them that's the only option.'

Callie drained her tea and stood up. 'Well,

that's your job, Daddy. You can tell them. I'm not getting involved in that discussion.'

'I'm happy to.' Braden stood and picked up both mugs and rinsed them in the sink. Are you right if I go out to the shed until Kent and Sophie arrive? Or do you want me to set the table or something?'

'You've put the table out near the barbeque, haven't you?'

'Yes. It's up.'

'You go to the shed and send the boys in on your way. They can set it while I put the salads together. Sophie and Kent won't be far away.'

Braden stood and caught Callie in a quick hug as she passed his chair. 'Why don't you go and have a quick lie down while the boys are setting the table? I can do the salads while Kent cooks the meat.'

'I'll think about it.'

Braden dropped a kiss on the end of her nose

and chuckled before he let Callie go and headed for the door.

'What? You don't trust me with a salad or two?'

CHAPTER 3

Sophie

Sophie waved back as Braden poked his head out the shed door and gave her a wave.

She turned to Kent. 'It's so good to see Braden so happy these days. He's been a different guy since he and Callie got married, hasn't he?'

'The best thing we ever did, all of us,' Kent said, squeezing her hand. 'Getting married.'

'And Ruby. She's the best thing too,' Sophie said, nodding her head toward the back seat where Ruby Rose was sound asleep in her car seat. 'I feel so silly now. All those doubts I had.'

'I think they're both pretty much an equal number one. Marriage and family.'

'They are, aren't they?' Sophie replied. Kent squeezed her hand again, and Sophie smiled as a wave of contentment washed over her. All those doubts she had about motherhood, about giving birth, about her ability to look after a baby, had disappeared the instant Dr Harry had placed Ruby Rose in her arms. A wave of love, unlike anything she had ever felt before, had consumed her as she looked down at the perfect little face of their baby girl. She'd looked up at Kent, and tears filled her eyes as she saw tears streaming down his cheeks. He gripped her hand and then leaned down and pressed his wet cheek to hers.

'We've done well, Kent.'

'*You've* done well,' he said.

And to think she'd been terrified of the labour. Ruby Rose had been born in just under two hours and Dr. Harry had been kept busy running between the labour ward where she was, and next door where Amelia Riley was giving birth to their little boy, Sebastian.

'I must catch up with Amelia this week,' she

said as Kent parked near the back fence of the house yard of *Kilcoy Station*. 'We've had a couple of quick phone chats and texts, but I must go into town for a visit.'

Kent honked the horn as he turned the motor off.

'Kent! You'll wake her up. And Megan and Munro!'

'Oops sorry, didn't think.' His smile was apologetic. 'I'm learning. This is only our second outing with her.'

A smile tilted Sophie's lips too as she heard the squeals and whooping as her three nephews ran over to the car.

'That's a welcome and a half,' she said.

Nigel was almost beside himself. His face was red, and he was jumping and punching the air with both fists.

'I'd see they're excited to see their new cousin for the first time.' Kent hurried out and came around to open Sophie's door. She held her hand out to him and smiled as he helped her out of the car.

Kent had always been a gentleman, but since her pregnancy had been confirmed, he'd been extra attentive. He squeezed her hand again before letting go and opening the back door. Ruby Rose was still sound asleep.

'Are you right to get her out while I give the boys a hug? And I'll tell them to be a little bit quieter.' Sophie whispered.

'I think I'll be right.'

Nigel rushed over and wrapped his arms around her legs. 'Aunty, Soph, it's so good you're here today.'

'It's good to see you too, Nigel,' she said quietly. 'Let's whisper so we don't wake Ruby Rose up. I guess you're all excited to see her.'

'We'll see her later. We need to talk to you. It's urgent.' Nigel dropped his voice to a loud whisper.

'Urgent?' Sophie frowned. 'What's wrong?'

'Don't you dare tell, Nigel!' Rory came racing behind, but his grin was as wide as his little brother's.

Petie brought up the rear, hugging his precious Apricot. Wherever Petie was, his dog, Apricot wasn't far away. Everyone had gotten used to the name Petie had chosen when they all got new pups when Callie first arrived at *Kilcoy Station*.

'We're really, really glad you're here,' Nigel said.

Rory put his finger to his lips. 'Shush, it's a secret, remember?'

'It's not a secret,' Nigel said with a smile. 'Don't be silly, Rory.'

Sophie raised her eyebrows.

'Okay, Rory said what *we're* doing is a secret; the project isn't. Everyone knows about that.'

'A secret?' Sophie asked. 'You three know I love secrets. Come on, I won't tell.'

Rory's grin grew wider. 'We just can't say what it is exactly, Nigel,' he said.

'Yes, but we still have to ask Aunty Sophie for permission. And the others.'

'Okay, you three come over here and sit on the swing with me and tell me what's going on.'

Kent was waiting by the car nursing Ruby. 'And then I'll have to help Uncle Kent get the stuff out of the car.'

Kent was cradling their baby close to his chest. 'When you're done, I'll come back out and get the stuff out of the back.'

'Not a problem. I just need to talk to the boys for a moment. I'll be in, in a while.'

Kent smiled and walked across to the back door. Callie must have heard the horn beep; the screen door was open almost immediately and

Kent disappeared inside.

'We've set the table for Mum,' Petie said proudly. 'We even put some candles out.'

'Good job,' Sophie said as she led them across to the swing set near the fence. It always warmed her heart to hear the boys call Callie "Mum". She was the best stepmother ever, not to mention a wonderful sister-in-law.

Rory sat beside her on the double swing, while Nigel and Petie stood next to them. 'You're pretty good at keeping secrets, Aunty Soph, I know that. But this one is a *special* secret.'

Petie started giggling, 'Aunty Soph, it's so funny, especially when the donkey farts.'

'A donkey?' Sophie burst out laughing. 'Have you got a donkey now? I didn't think your dad would ever agree to that.'

Braden had never been a lover of horses, but when Julia, his first wife and the boys' mother had died in a horse accident, he'd switched the property to aerial and motorbike mustering.

'No, it's an imaginary donkey,' Petie said. 'You know that.'

'I don't know what's going on at all. I don't know what this project is. And I don't know what the donkey's got to do with anything, but I think you need to tell me.'

'You have to promise,' Nigel said.

'Okay, guys, I cross my heart. I won't tell anyone what's going on.' Sophie wondered if she was promising too readily. Knowing these three, they could be up to all sorts of mischief.

'Well,' Nigel and Rory both tried to speak at the same time.

'No, Nigel. I'm the oldest so I get to ask.' Rory shoved Nigel as he leaned close to Sophie.

'Settle down,' she said.

'Alright.' Nigel's lip dropped, a mannerism that was very familiar to Sophie from when she'd looked after the boys for eighteen months after Julia had died.

Rory rushed on. 'Mrs Jansen and Miss Riordan have got us—'

'Writing,' Nigel interrupted.

'And it's for Christmas,' Petie said, not to be outdone.

'One at a time,' Sophie said. 'Rory, you go first.'

'Well, Miss Riordan, she's my teacher. You know her.'

'Yes, I know her very well. She's a good friend of mine, and I know she's a very good teacher. So, she's given you something to do, has she?'

'Not exactly,' Nigel said. 'Now it's my turn. Mrs Jansen, *my* new teacher who is really super-duper, had the idea and Miss Riordan made it a project for the whole school and she's given us the same project. It's a competition and anyone can enter.'

'What do you have to do?' Sophie asked.

Nigel rushed in to speak before Rory could answer. 'You have to write a play. You can write it by yourself, or in a group, but it has to be controversial. But still be about Christmas. And Mary and Joseph and joy and all that sort of stuff.'

'And the donkey. Don't forget the donkey,' Petie chimed in.

Sophie raised her eyebrows. 'Controversial?'

Rory shook his head. 'No, no. You know what the nativity play is, don't you?'

'Yes, I do. I was in one every year I was at your primary school.'

'Well, we have to write a nativity story, but it has to be different. Mrs Jansen and Miss Riordan said it can be the nativity stuff that we always do, or it can be set now. It doesn't have to be in the olden times when Mary was on the real donkey.'

Sophie said, 'Maybe she meant contemporary.'

'Yes, that's exactly what it was,' Rory said. 'I remember that word. She wrote it on the board. So, see, Nigel, you got it wrong, you have to let me explain.' Rory nodded, like the grown-up ten-year-old he was. 'It has to have a theme.'

Nigel pouted and kicked his bare foot in the dirt underneath the swing set.

'Stop pouting, Nigel,' Sophie said from habit. 'And what does the theme have to be, boys?'

'Okay,' Rory said. 'It has to be something special about families, something special about love, and something about Christmas.'

'About joy,' Nigel added.

'That leaves it pretty open.' Sophie couldn't help the grin that crossed her face. 'Again, now tell me, boys, so that's where the donkey is. It's not a real one. So, tell me how you're going to do the story with love and happiness and joy in it?'

'Well, we thought we'd keep the original story about a man and a lady getting married and having a baby,' Rory explained.

Nigel rushed in. 'Because everybody in Augathella is so happy, and we know it's all because they found who they wanted to marry. And we could still have Joseph and Mary and the baby, and the donkey too.'

'It sounds very creative.' Sophie nodded slowly. 'Yeah, I get your drift.'

'There was Dad and Callie first.'

Nigel chimed in. 'And then you and Uncle Kent. And Fallon and Jon.'

'My turn,' Petie said.

Sophie turned to Petie. 'Do you want to add anyone?'

Little Petie beamed. 'Yes. Ben and Amelia and Chilli Girl.'

Sophie nodded, getting into the swing of their

idea. 'I like it.'

'And then there was Nurse Bec and Matt, who saved me at your wedding,' Petie said. 'Mum said they're getting married soon.'

'And then there was Miss Riordan and Mr Calthorpe.' Nigel squealed as his excitement built. 'And Dr. Harry and the nurse who gave Mum the twins.'

'And don't forget Aunty Jacinta and Uncle Ryder,' Rory chimed in.

'Well, you've certainly got a handle on things,' Sophie said. 'We have a busy town, haven't we? And you're right, everybody's happy. So how are you going to show this in the Christmas play?'

'Nigel had the best idea,' Rory said grinning at his little brother.

'Well, I thought we could have Mary near the manger, and then the narrator—'

'What narrator?' Sophie asked.

'Well, because we've only got a week, there's no lines for the cast to learn. The narrator, probably Mrs Jansen, will do all the talking.'

'Except for the donkey,' Nigel squealed.

'Anyway,' Rory continued, 'she could read our script about joy, and some of the kids could play all the happy people we said before. They don't have to talk, just walk through on the stage and Mrs Jansen would say their name.'

'It works for me; except do you mean a real donkey or a pretend one?'

'A pretend one. Rory and I want to be the donkey.'

Rory, Nigel and Petie all screamed with laughter.

Sophie shrugged. 'I guess it would be funny being a pretend donkey.'

The boys kept laughing.

'So much fun,' Rory screamed. 'And I get to be the back end of the donkey.'

Sophie nodded slowly, enjoying the boys' mirth. 'Sounds good to me, but you know you'll have to check with all those friends to make sure they're okay with being in a play?'

'Yes, we can do that at the pub next weekend. We've made a list,' Rory said. 'And we can ring up Aunty Jacinta.'

'Well done, guys. It sounds good to me.' Sophie jumped off the swing. 'Now, come and meet your new cousin.'

The boys looked at each other.

'Um, there's one more thing,' Rory said.

'This is what we really, really needed to talk to you about. And remember, it's a big secret. You don't know anything we told you,' Nigel reminded.

'Okay, so what do you need me for?'

'Well, seeing we've got a new cousin, we thought she could be in our play.'

Sophie's eyes widened. 'I only know of one

new cousin that you've got. And Uncle Kent just carried her inside. How do you expect Ruby to be in your play? She's a bit little.'

'We thought when they ride us—I mean, the donkey—into the hall, she could be in the basket of straw on the stage. And if somebody poked her, she could cry, because if she's in the basket of straw, they won't be able to see her from down in the audience. We haven't really figured that one out yet,' Rory explained.

'We could put her near the curtain and you could stand behind it, and reach around and poke her, Aunty Soph,' Nigel said.

'Hmm, I'll have to have a good think about that, boys. Now I'd better go and say hello to your mum and dad.'

'And remember, it's a secret,' Rory said. 'Everything.'

'Okay, but seeing Uncle Kent will be in the play, can I tell him I gave you my permission.'

Rory put his finger to his lip.' What do you think, Nigel?'

Sophie kept a straight face while Nigel considered the question for a moment.

'I think you can tell him. We can trust Uncle Kent.'

'Thank you. I'll swear him to secrecy too. I think what you guys need to do is get this written down, and then I can have a read of it. And then we'll talk about Ruby Rose again. Got a deal?'

She held up a hand for a high-five and got a high-five from Rory and Nigel, while Petie grinned.

'Looks like you've got a deal, Aunty Soph,' Petie said.

CHAPTER 4

Sophie

Sophie smiled as she opened the screen door and walked into Callie's kitchen. Kent was over at the sink filling the kettle, and Callie was sitting at the table nursing Ruby Rose.

'Hi, Cal,' Sophie said with a wide smile as Callie looked up.

'Hi, Soph. How are you? You look amazing.' Callie had shadows beneath her eyes.

'Really good.'

'I hear she's sleeping well.' Callie looked down at her new niece.

'Has Kent been bragging? He's a besotted new dad. But yes, Ruby's the opposite of what I was expecting. She's slept through from eight till six the last three nights.'

Kent switched the kettle on. 'I'll leave you

41

pair to chat. I'll go and see if Braden's got any cold beer in the shed.'

'Half your luck,' Callie said with a tired smile. 'The twins are still waking twice each night at different times.'

'I don't know how you do it, Callie. And you've gone back to work one day a week.'

'That's my holiday. It's the day when Braden deals with all the nappies and the washing and the feeding, and the bottle sterilising. I quite enjoy my Mondays at school,' she said.

'Well, if you ever need a hand, yell out. I'm happy to come over.'

'I might hold you to that when the mustering starts,' Callie said. 'What did the boys want? You looked like you had some secret business going on out there. The huddle on the swings.'

Sophie tapped her nose. 'Definitely secret business. I promised I wouldn't tell.'

'Sounds like they're up to mischief again,' Callie said. 'They've been hyper and laughing all afternoon.'

'No, the opposite actually. They were talking to me about a school project, and that's all I can say.'

'Ah, the nativity play,' Callie said.

'You know about it?'

'I know what the topic is. It's Emily Jansen's idea.'

'They said Mrs Jansen. Do I know her? I guess she's the new teacher at school. She's not been in town long, has she? Or is she the one with the little girl with the pretty name?'

'Ophelia, and yes, Emily is the best, one of the best teachers we've ever had, and the kids absolutely adore her.'

'That's good to hear.'

'Anyway, Nigel's had her this term, and he's absolutely smitten. He comes home every

43

afternoon he has her: "Mrs Jansen said this" and "Mrs Jansen did that." Makes me feel quite inadequate as a mum and a teacher,' Callie said.

'I think I met her at dinner at the pub.'

'Yes, she joined our group one night. She's living at Jenna's place. She knows Luke Elliot, the guy from— oh, hang on, you know Luke. He works with Kent at your place too, doesn't he?'

'Yeah, I know Luke. I thought he and Jenna were going out.'

'Where have you been for the last few weeks?'

Sophie chuckled. 'At home with a newborn baby. I've only been to town once so far, and I was inundated. Every second person wanted to see her, poke her and talk to her, cuddle her, kiss and hug her.' She shook her head. 'She's little. I'm staying away from crowds.'

'It doesn't actually get that crowded in town,' Callie said.

'No, but you can still get germs from one or two people. Let me get her to a few months older, and then I might start socialising a bit more.'

'Are you coming to the pub for our Christmas dinner next Sunday?'

'I'll think about it,' Sophie said. 'Okay, tell me what's going on. What have I missed?'

'Well, Jenna's left the tea rooms for a while. She put it in Ella's care for a couple of weeks, and she's gone away with—wait for it—Amelia Riley's brother.'

'Amelia's brother? Do I know him?'

'No, he came to town, and he and Jenna . . . wow. Do you believe in love at first sight? It was instant,' Callie said. 'So, Jenna's gone back to North Queensland with him for a visit. I hear she's coming back soon though. And I've heard that he's buying a place around here.'

'Poor Luke,' Sophie said. 'I thought he was quite taken with Jenna.'

Callie shook her head. 'We all thought that but I think we were wrong. I don't think "taken" was the word. I think if you saw him with Emily, you'd understand what I'm talking about.'

'He's certainly a quiet guy. He hasn't said a word about any of this when he's been out with Kent. Very private.'

'So, back to Emily, anyway. She's a lovely person and a lovely teacher. She's very quiet too. She often doesn't look happy. I think she might have a bit of a past that's sent her flying out here. Anyway, it's none of our business, so let's get back to this nativity plan. Emily and Kimberley have set the topic, and whoever writes the best play gets to pick the cast, but even if it is set in the present, there has to be a Mary and Joseph.'

Sophie chuckled. 'And a donkey.' Callie looked at her curiously. 'I don't know anything about donkeys. I just know that when the guys have been out there making up the story, they have been in absolute hysterics.'

'I can understand why,' Sophie tapped her nose. 'You'll see.'

CHAPTER 5

Emily

As Emily Jansen walked across the playground of the primary school, her name was called.

'Mrs Jansen, Mrs Jansen!'

She turned with a smile, which grew as the three Cartwright boys ran across the grass towards her.

'Good morning, Rory, Nigel, and Petie. You're having another orientation day here today, Petie, I believe.'

'Yes, Mrs Jansen, we're going to do some Christmas decorations today, Miss Kimberley said. But I already know how to make them because Mum teaches us at home, so I'll be able to help the other children.'

'That would be a good help, Petie.' Emily

nodded as she walked towards her classroom. 'Now, was that just a good morning you were calling out to me before, or did you want something?'

She stopped walking as Rory put his finger to his lips.

'Can we ask you a private question?' he said.

'As long as it doesn't break the rules,' Nigel added.

'What rules, Nigel?' Emily asked.

'Well, it's about the play project and the rules.'

She nodded and looked at them. 'Yes?'

'We've started to write the play, and it's really, really good.' Rory nodded seriously.

Petie was jumping around. 'It makes me laugh, it's so funny. I've got two very smart brothers.'

'That's wonderful to hear. So, what's your question about the rules, boys?'

Nigel looked around again to make sure there were no other children near them, and Emily smiled. Many children were taking this play competition seriously, with groups sitting together in the playground with pencils and paper every lunchtime since she and Kimberley had announced the competition.

'Our literacy engagement has really improved,' Kimberley had said the other day. 'All thanks to you, Emily. You've certainly hit the sweet spot with this one.'

'No, I'm sure you've done it before, and literacy here is good already. I've looked at your data, and the school is already above the benchmark for rural schools. And I've worked in other schools where there hasn't been the enthusiasm that the teachers here have,' she said.

Kimberley had already spoken to her about work next year, and Emily was seriously considering it. It was a wonderful school, with well-behaved children and fabulous staff.

Ruth had indicated she was available to mind Ophelia next year, and Jenna was happy to have them stay in the apartment for as long as she needed it.

Emily frowned; the sticking point for her was Luke, but she'd think about that later. She turned back to the boys.

'Okay, we don't have many rules, but is there one in particular that you want to ask about?'

Rory put his hand up as his brothers both started to talk.

'Petie, you're not in this; you're just the audience. Nigel, I'm the oldest so let me check with Mrs Jansen.'

Nigel's face fell. 'But it was my idea.'

'Doesn't matter if it was your idea; if it doesn't fit the rules, we can't use it.'

'I'm not sure if I can answer you. If your

question gives you an advantage, it might be unfair to the other children. How about I just go through the rules with you, and then you can make up your mind if you still need to ask me?'

'Yeah, that's what Mum said too. It's okay,' Nigel said. 'She read the rules last night, so we're just gonna have to wing it. If we do it wrong, that's our bad luck.'

Emily smothered a smile and nodded. "Wing it" sounded good.

'Well, I'm really looking forward to reading your play when you get it finished, boys. And as long as you are aware of the rules—which it sounds as though you are— and follow them, you won't be disqualified. I'm sure it will be a very good story.'

Petie burst out laughing. 'It sure is, Mrs Jansen, it is the funniest story. You see, there is this donkey—'

Nigel leaned over and put his hand over his

brother's mouth. 'Petie, shut up. Don't talk about it, and don't you dare tell any of the other kids today anything about it. If you do, I'm going to go and see Mum, and she'll put you in the car, and you can sit there all day.'

Emily shook her head. 'I don't think that would be wise, Nigel, putting anyone in a car. And I'm sure Petie won't tell.'

'You better not,' Nigel's eyes narrowed, glaring at his little brother.

'Well, boys, you have a good day. I'll see you in class, Nigel. I'm going to get our classroom ready for the day. I can't wait to read your play. Remember, it's due this Friday.'

'Yes, we know that. We're just tidying up now. We've got our story done. It's just a question we had about the characters and permissions,' he said. 'But we won't ask you. We won't get an advantage over the other kids.'

They ran off to the playground where their

friends were already playing on the equipment in the soft-fall area.

Emily smiled as she headed towards the classroom. Gladys was walking down the corridor and looked at her with a frown.

'Good morning, Mrs. Tingle, can I help you?'

Gladys Tingle usually volunteered in the canteen a couple of days a week. 'It's alright, Mrs Jansen. Sylvia is sick today, so I've been doing the cleaning for her. Your classroom is ready, and may I say what a beautiful classroom you have. I didn't have to pick up any paper or sweep the floor like I have to with—'

Emily put up her hand and interrupted before she had to listen to a "name and shame" session. 'Thank you for that. I'm so pleased that you found it easy. Anyway, I have to get ready for the day so I need a few minutes. It's only twenty minutes to the bell time. Thank you so much for coming in and helping out; we really appreciate it.'

She turned before she could get involved in one of the gossip sessions Gladys Tingle was notorious for; she had often tried to waylay Emily when she was on playground duty or canteen.

As she put out the pencils and writing pads for the first numeracy session this morning, her mind turned to Luke; she'd been stunned when she first came to town to discover that he was working in Augathella, flying in and working on a lot of the properties. Since he'd learned she was now here for the three months of next term as well, he based himself in the town and was flying out to his other Queensland properties and Northern Territory jobs with his base at Augathella. She hadn't told him yet that it was likely she would be here for the whole of the next school year.

The last time he came around to the apartment, Emily had found it hard to resist him and had to remind herself why she wasn't resuming a relationship with Luke Elliott. No matter how much she wanted to, no matter how attractive she found him, and no matter how much she knew deep down that she loved him, and she always had, she couldn't trust herself.

The loss of her husband and their strained relationship had left Emily with doubts that she would ever be able to maintain a relationship.

No matter what a lovely person Luke was, she still knew that the chance she would stuff it up was there; so, no matter how much he pushed she was not going to listen to him.

A pang of envy had hit her chest when she'd seen the boys tumble out of Callie's car. Ophelia was never going to have any brothers and sisters and she would always be the only child of a single parent.

Emily vowed to herself that she would be the best single mother in the world. Ophelia would *not* suffer because of her determination to remain single. She would resist Luke Elliott, no matter how hard he tried to convince her that they were meant to be together.

Perhaps they were, but Emily would never be in a position to commit.

CHAPTER 6

Emily

Emily stood in front of the mirror, focusing her attention on the hair curler as she curled strands of hair on each side of her face. It had been three years since she had last been to a Christmas party, and she was looking forward to it.

Thank goodness that she found Ruth.

Ruth was the most wonderful woman, and Emily was sure that Ophelia was already starting to think of her as her surrogate grandma. A pang of sadness ran through her. Her parents had both passed away when she was in her teens; she had been a change-of-life baby to parents in their forties. When Ophelia was born, Troy's mother, now living in America with her second husband, had shown little interest in her new granddaughter, having already had another three grandchildren from Troy's step-siblings. Emily closed her mind to Troy's reaction to his child; she couldn't bear to go there.

If Ruth was prepared to fill the role of grandma for a few months, Emily was more than happy to let her.

'Mama, mama,' a little voice called from the living room.

Emily put the hair curler down, picked up her lipstick, and gave her lips a second coat of the pastel pink colour. She pulled out the new summer dress. New from the ops shop, anyway.

Tonight, she almost felt like a princess as she dropped the soft silk dress over her head and slipped into the strappy sandals she'd bought at the same op shop in Charleville.

She walked into the living room where Ophelia was playing happily on the floor, making a tower of blocks and knocking them down. 'Mama, pretty,' she said.

'Thank you, my sweetie, and so are you,' Emily had dressed Ophelia in the new dress she'd picked up at the bargain store in Charleville. Surprisingly, it was a kids' label brand and fitted perfectly.

Since Emily was going out for dinner, she had decided to dress Ophelia up for her visit to Ruth's house. She'd also packed some shorts, T-shirts, and her sleeping suit into the bag along with her bottles.

'Come on, bubs, it's time to go and see Auntie Ruth.'

Ophelia's little face lit up as Emily reached down and scooped her off the floor. She put her bag in the back of the car and headed two streets away to Ruth's house.

##

As the school had quite a large number of staff, the group tonight including partners, cleaning staff, and teachers' aides filled the private dining room at the hotel. Emily sat at the side of the table, her heart thudding.

When she'd walked through the bistro to the private dining room, her eyes had widened as she spotted Luke Elliott sitting at a table for four with an unfamiliar woman.

Luke had his back to her, but Emily would recognise him anywhere. She put her head down and hurried through the bistro into the dining room, wondering why Luke was there and who he was with. She had gotten to know most of the people in town in her few weeks here, but the woman was unfamiliar.

She shrugged and focused on staying calm; it didn't matter. She had made her intentions clear to Luke; no matter how much he insisted they should resume their relationship from several years ago, Emily had stayed firm. It didn't matter what she felt. It didn't matter that she wanted to accept Luke's offer and ride into the sunset with him for a happily ever after because she knew there wouldn't be one.

Anyway, she wasn't going to think about Luke Elliott being there tonight, or who he was with. She was here to have a good time in the company of her new workmates. She really liked the staff at Augathella Primary School, and when Bob Hamblin had called her in last Friday and raised the possibility of a whole year of work next year, Emily had accepted readily without even having to think about it.

Only a couple of the staff had arrived before her. Emily liked to be early because she could pick where she was sitting. So now, she sat with her back to the door where she wouldn't be tempted to look out to see if she could see Luke.

Kimberley Riordan was sitting opposite her, looking at her phone. After a few seconds, she put it down and smiled over at Emily.

'Sorry, Emily. Just reminding Quinn to get here as soon as he can. Don't you look gorgeous! Amazing how we all brush up for Christmas, isn't it?' Kimberley reached into a bag beside her chair and pulled out a circle of green tinsel. 'We decided not to inflict Christmas hats on the staff this year, so we've got tinsel circlets for the ladies and tinsel ties for the gentlemen.'

Emily reached over with a smile and placed the circle of tinsel carefully on her head. 'Your hair looks gorgeous,' Kimberley said. 'Such a pretty colour.'

'Thank you. It was fun getting dressed up tonight. I haven't done that for a long time.'

Kimberley looked at her curiously, and Emily knew that the whole town wondered about her background. She'd trusted Luke not to tell anyone, and she hadn't shared it with anyone. She and Ruth had had a bit of a talk one night, and she told Ruth that she was now a widow, but she asked Ruth to honour her privacy and not tell anyone, and she knew she could trust the older woman. She hadn't shared any of the details with Ruth; it was hard enough to carry them, let alone verbalise them

Gradually, the rest of the staff arrived, and soon the dining room was a hubbub of noise, laughter, and conversation. Bob Hamblin took pride of place at the head of the table, and at the far end sat Gladys Tingle, who had been doing some casual cleaning; as far as Emily could see, Gladys didn't miss a trick.

Emily smothered a smile. The older woman had tried over and over again, calling into Kimberley and Emily's classroom, to pry out some details about Emily, but Emily was an expert at deflecting her questions.

Callie and Braden Cartwright took the two chairs on Kimberley's left and smiled at Emily as they sat down. 'Hi, Emily. It's good to see you. We saw Ophelia at Ruth's when we dropped the boys and the twins off.'

'Ruth is amazing, isn't she?' Emily said.

Callie nodded. 'She sure is, but we won't be having a late night.'

'Neither will I,' Emily agreed. 'Although sometimes I think Ophelia would be happy to live with Ruth. She gets upset when we leave now. I think our room is pretty boring. Ruth has so many toys at her place.'

'She's minded so many children over the last twelve months she's gathered quite a collection of toys,' Callie said.

A man who Emily hadn't seen before walked along the other side of the table, stopped, and put his hand on Braden Cartwright's shoulder. 'Gidday, Braden. Good to see you.'

Braden looked up, and his smile was wide. 'Hey, Quinn! Haven't seen you for ages. Good thing our girls work at the school, and we see each other at least once a year.'

Kimberley leaned over towards Emily and caught her attention. 'Emily, this is my fiancé, Quinn. Quinn, this is Emily Jansen, the new teacher at the school.'

'Hello, Quinn. It's nice to meet you.' she said. He was a nice-looking guy, and Emily smiled when she saw him take hold of Kimberley's hand.

How sweet.

A pang of envy lodged in her chest and Emily pushed it away. She was here to have a good time. Not to brood on what could have been.

Or what could be, an insistent little voice said in her head.

'Emily, we're not going to talk work tonight,' Callie said. 'But I just wanted to ask you whether Rory and Nigel caught up with you. They've been asking me so many questions about the Christmas play. I told them to go and see you at lunchtime yesterday.'

Emily nodded and smiled. 'Yes, they came to be before school, but then decided not to ask me the question, because they didn't want to have an unfair advantage.'

Callie shook her head. 'They're taking this so seriously.'

'I mentioned the rules of the task to them, and they both said they understood. That you'd told them.'

Braden rolled his eyes. 'How do you do it, Emily? They rarely listen to a word I say.'

'Right,' Callie said. 'That's it. No more work talk.'

Kimberley turned to Callie. 'I hear you guys might be going away for a trip before Christmas.'

Emily was surprised to see alarm cross Callie's face as she shot a swift glance at Braden.

'Yes, we're going down to the Gold Coast

for four days to take the boys to the theme parks before Christmas. They don't know yet. How did you hear?' Callie asked.

'Um, Gladys.' Kimberley lowered her voice. 'Are you taking them out of school?' Kimberley asked.

'For the last couple of days because the term ends in the middle of the week,' Braden said. 'Callie will be finished for the year and we've got such a busy schedule, we've decided to go down and be home for Christmas.'

'Does that mean that you won't be in town for the play, Callie?' Kimberley asked glumly.

'Looks like it, but we haven't broken the news to the boys yet.'

'Oh dear, they will be a bit disappointed,' Emily said. 'But the appeal of Sea World and Dreamworld should make up for it.'

Callie shook her head slowly. 'I'm starting to wonder. We haven't mentioned it yet, so we'll see what the reaction is.'

'Petie will be fine,' Braden said. 'He's absolutely fixated on Nemo.'

The conversation drifted from one topic to another as the entrees were served. Emily's ears pricked up when Kimberley asked Callie a question.

'Who's that out there with Jenna and Josh?' Kimberley asked.

'Jenna? I didn't see her out there,' Callie replied. 'I didn't think they were back. I thought they were up in the Gulf of Carpentaria at his parents' place.'

'No, they flew in this afternoon,' Quinn said. 'I was out near the airport getting some Avgas for my plane, and Josh flew in. He had another two women with him, too. So, they've obviously got guests.'

Kimberley chuckled. 'Nothing is private in this town, is it?'

'No, we've got a pretty good grapevine going.' Callie rolled her eyes and gestured down towards the end of the table where Gladys was chatting to two of the teachers' aides. 'With some help.'

'And that grapevine has certainly had a hold on the school for the last couple of weeks. How on earth did she know about your holiday?' Kimberley said.

Callie rolled her eyes as well. 'No idea. She's one for gossip, that's for sure, but she's got a heart of gold. I hope Gladys hasn't been pestering you, Emily.'

Emily gave an absent smile. 'I can handle myself,' she said, wondering who Jenna's guests were, and if it was the woman she had seen sitting with Luke.

Putting down her fork, she picked up her napkin and dabbed at her cheeks. It was awfully hot in here, but there was no way she was going to walk out and draw attention to herself. She swallowed a few times as the conversations around her merged into an unbearable noise; by sheer will, she forced back the building panic attack.

CHAPTER 7

Emily

Later that night

It was a lovely warm evening with a cool breeze blowing from the northeast. So far, the weather hadn't been as hot as she'd expected out here, even though it was the beginning of summer.

The weather had been under discussion tonight, and everyone had agreed that it was pleasantly cool for this time of the year. Emily didn't mind the heat. In fact, she welcomed the dry heat of the west after living in the humidity of the northern tropics for three years. That was the heat she couldn't cope with.

Pushing the stroller to Ruth's had been a good idea, and Emily had been able to have two wines—one before dinner and a champagne to toast Christmas with the girls after they finished their meal. The wine had relaxed her and she had enjoyed herself, and again she thanked her luck in getting a position at a school with such kind and caring staff.

The only difficult part of the night had been knowing that Luke was sitting outside the dining room. She'd managed to get over the panic attack before it took hold, and had focused on talking to everyone at the table, as they moved around between courses. At dessert, she found herself sitting on the other side of the table looking out into the bistro, but to her relief, there'd been no sign of Luke and the group he was dining with.

It would have been much better if she hadn't had him in her thoughts as she sat back and listened to the conversations wash around her. If she was going to make a success of her new life, it would be better if Luke hadn't encountered her that first night at Jenna's unit.

With him in town for long-term stays and the

chance of bumping into him—not to mention the three occasions he had knocked on her door in the last two weeks—made it very difficult for Emily to move on, and she needed to move on.

She turned the stroller around the corner into Jenna's, not surprised to see the light on in the front room of the apartment block. Listening to the talk at the table, she suspected Jenna would be home by the time she'd picked Ophelia up and walked home.

As long as Luke wasn't there too.

Ophelia had been asleep when she arrived at Ruth's to pick her up, and she had managed to transfer her from the small cot into the stroller without her waking. 'She's had a lovely evening,' Ruth said. 'I hope it was alright to let her stay up till seven thirty because she was having so much fun playing with the Cartwright boys. She was fascinated with Ryan too and kept pointing at him, saying "Bubba". She's really started to talk since you've been in town.'

'Yes, I've noticed that too. Her vocabulary has expanded in the last three weeks.'

Emily walked slowly along the street, enjoying the fresh air, the crescent moon hanging low in the east, and the stars brilliant in the indigo sky. Three doors up from the apartment block, she heard footsteps crunching on the gravel path behind her but wasn't overly concerned. She already knew that Augathella was a safe place to be out at night.

'Emily, wait up.'

She kept walking and briefly closed her eyes, ignoring Luke's request as she gripped the handles of the stroller.

'Emily, it's me, Luke. I didn't mean to give you a fright.'

There was no need for him to say that; she knew very well who it was. Huffing a sigh, Emily stopped walking but kept pushing the stroller backward and forwards; the last thing she wanted was for Ophelia to wake up. If she woke up this early in the night, she'd be up for hours wanting to play, and after having a couple of wines, Emily was more than ready for her bed.

'Luke,' she said, keeping her voice expressionless.

'Hi, Emily. I was watching for you to leave the pub, but I missed you. By the time I saw the last of your group leave and the lights went out in the dining room I realised I hadn't seen you walk out.'

'Yes, you must've missed me,' she said, not letting on that she'd slipped out through the back door of the dining room, which led directly onto the street, for this very reason; she hadn't wanted to have a conversation with Luke tonight.

'Did you have a good time? There was lots of laughter coming from the dining room. I was in the bistro with Jenna and Josh, and some of his family.'

'I did. I went down to Ruth's to pick Ophelia up.'

'She's sound asleep,' Luke said, looking into the front of the stroller.

'Yes, and I don't want to wake her up, so I'm going to have to be rude and keep walking while we talk.'

'That's fine. I'm pleased you enjoyed yourself, Em,' His voice was like a warm caress but Emily refused to react.

'How long are you in town for? Have you been away?' she asked

'Yes, I flew home for a couple of days last weekend just after I saw you. I was hoping that you'd come out and have dinner with me one night next week.'

'I'm pretty busy at school,' she said.

'Please don't make me beg.'

'Luke, I'm sorry. There's no point in us

seeing each other all the time. It's good to have you here, but I told you I just want to be friends. I want to put all of my energy into my job and establishing myself at the school and in town.'

Luke's face closed, and he was quiet for a moment. 'Very well. I won't hassle you. Good night, Emily.' He turned on his heel and began to walk away, and a surge of guilt rose into her throat.

'Luke,' she called after him. 'Come back.'

Luke stopped and walked towards her slowly. She stopped walking, and Ophelia didn't move or make a peep.

'I'm sorry, Luke. It's too soon. I know you want to pick up where we left off, but I've told you all we have is friendship.'

Luke's voice was ragged and it took all of Emily's self-control to stay strong.

How easy would it be to step into the safe haven of Luke's arms and let him care for her?

'That night when I came to you three weeks ago, that night that you let me hold you in my arms, you said we'd talk.'

'I know I did, Luke. The time's not been right. Like I said, I'm trying to sort myself out and settle down in town and at school. Perhaps you could be patient with me.'

'When will the time be right?'

Emily shrugged.

'How about if we go out for dinner as friends and we just have a conversation about what's happening in town and about your new job? Would that be acceptable to you?'

'Let me think about it, and I'll have to see if Ruth is available too. She's pretty busy with all the Christmas shows on at the moment, minding children from all over town.'

'I don't mind if you bring Ophelia. In fact, I'd love you to bring her.'

Well, there goes my last excuse, Emily

thought. She bit her lip. 'What night would suit you best?'

Luke's eyes lit up; hope gleamed in his moonlit eyes. 'You choose whatever would suit you best. I'm in your hands,' he said.

'Okay, well, this is my only Christmas function, apart from the picnic we have on the last day of school in just over two weeks, and I'll be tired that night. How about Sunday night of next weekend?'

'It's a date.' Luke reached over and squeezed the hand that was gripping the stroller. 'I look forward to it.'

Emily was tempted to repeat his words because she would look forward to it too, but she shook her head. There was no point in giving Luke any encouragement at all. 'I'll meet you at the pub that night at six o'clock, okay?'

'Six o'clock is fine. How about I pick you up?'

'No, I'll walk and meet you there. Ophelia will need a baby seat.' Emily frowned. 'If you're flying in and staying at the pub, how are you getting around?'

Luke pointed to his feet. 'I fly out to the properties and walk everywhere in town. Sometimes I bunk out at the properties, but Sean at the pub has been great. He's taken a permanent booking from me for a couple of months. I meant I'd come down and walk you to the pub.'

'Oh, okay. If you want to.'

Luke was whistling as he turned and walked back in the direction of the pub.

Emily wondered whether it was wise to have dinner with Luke; she'd see how that night went and she could make it clear to him that it was their one and only night out together.

Parking the stroller at the bottom of the steps, she undid the clasp on the front, gently lifted Ophelia out and put her on her shoulder.

She stood there until her little girl settled again.

As she waited for Ophelia's head to go back down to her shoulder; the noise of several different voices drifted out of the open window at the front of Jenna's living room.

Jenna and Joshua had been gone for two weeks, going home to Joshua's family station up in the country of North Queensland. Emily had been envious; Josh and Jenna had fallen hard and fast for each other, and Emily was so happy for them. It had been a delight to watch their relationship bloom over a few days.

She had enjoyed the last two weeks in the apartment by herself, and she had decided, once she signed a contract for the twelve months' work next year—and Bob Hamblin, the principal, had assured her that it would be ready early next week to sign—she would start looking for an apartment of her own.

At the moment, especially with Jenna and

Joshua coming home, she felt like a bit of a third wheel. She was sure Jenna would now prefer to have her apartment to herself, even though she told Emily she was welcome to stay as long as she wanted.

She pushed the stroller underneath the side of the carport; it didn't look like it was going to rain, and there was no fear of anyone taking it in the short time it would take to put Ophelia down.

She walked up the stairs, and the front door was open as she turned left off the porch. She hesitated for a moment, unsure whether to knock and then decided just to open the screen door and go in. It was her home too; she was paying rent to Jenna. She opened the door and walked quietly to the large archway that opened into the living room.

Jenna and Josh were sitting on the sofa, and an older woman and a young woman were sitting on the other double sofa facing them. Jenna jumped up, but Emily put her fingers to her lips and nodded to Ophelia sleeping on her shoulder.

'I'll come back out in a few minutes,' she said quietly. Jenna sat back down, and Emily walked down the hall, opened her bedroom door, and rocked her daughter for a little while until she was sure she was sound asleep. She put her in the cot, felt her nappy to make sure she was dry, and then lightly pulled the sheet up over her little shoulders.

Emily looked down, and a wave of love for her child ran through her as she ran her fingers gently through her soft curls. She took a quick trip to the bathroom, and when she was in there, she fluffed up her hair and reapplied her lipstick. If Jenna had guests, she might as well look presentable.

She walked down the hallway, hearing laughter, and her spirits lifted as she realised how she had heard very little apart from laughter in the weeks she'd been in town. Everything had been happy and laughter surrounded her every day. The children at the school had been wonderful and accepted a new teacher at this late time of the year without a problem. Her class was delightful, and she'd taken to it like a duck to water.

She walked into the living room, and Jenna smiled. 'Come and join us, Emily, come and meet Josh's family.'

'Josh's family?' she asked curiously.

The older woman waved to her from the sofa. 'Hello, Emily. We've heard all about you. I'm Josh's mum, Lucy Foley.'

'Hello, it's nice to meet you, Lucy.'

The young woman jumped up. 'I'm Molly. Molly Foley.' Emily frowned. She didn't think, from what Jen and Josh told her, that Josh had any sisters. But the young woman rushed on to explain. 'I'm Josh's brother's wife. We live in

Darwin, and Josh brought Jenna up to meet us, and seeing Amelia has had her baby, Mum and I decided to come down and surprise her.'

She shot an affectionate glance at her mother-in-law. 'But the surprise was on us. Would you believe that Ben and Amelia have gone down to Charleville for the weekend? His mother went down with them, visiting some of Ben's family down there. They're just away for the night, and apparently, they'll be back tomorrow afternoon.'

'That will be a lovely surprise for them. I'm sure they'll be absolutely delighted to see you. I know Amelia misses being home. I had a good chat with her at the spring fair. She was really sad her family wouldn't be here for her new baby.'

'We're here and we're so looking forward to seeing Amelia. I'm not going to sleep a wink tonight,' Lucy said. 'Family is the most important thing there is.'

CHAPTER 8

Amelia

'I'll have to mow the lawn this afternoon,' Ben said as he changed back a gear and turned into their driveway.

'Sounds good, we might put the Christmas lights up. What's your mum up to for the rest of the weekend?'

'She's got the CWA Christmas party tonight. She's still busy putting out the last of the Christmas cakes for the CWA. I think they've got a stall in town a couple of mornings this week. Why do you ask?'

'Oh, no reason. I know what a busy life she leads. It was lovely of her to come to Charleville with us to see your extended family.'

It had been nice to meet Ben's cousins and aunts and uncles, but it had brought home to

Amalei how much she missed her family.

Ben reached over and squeezed her hand as he parked in the carport, picking up on her mood as he always did. 'You're a good daughter-in-law, Amelia. You're very thoughtful.'

'I love your mum,' she said. 'She's a great mum-in-law and your dad too, of course.'

They had only been inside for a few minutes, and Amelia had changed Seb's nappy. She was about to put him into the cot when she heard steps come up the front stairs and voices at the door.

'Ben, can you get that? There's someone at the front door. I'm just about to put Sebastian down in the cot.'

'Don't you dare put him in the cot yet.' Josh's voice called from the front door.

'Josh, Jenna, come on in. Okay, I'll bring him down. He can go for a little snooze after you have a cuddle.'

Amelia walked down the hall with their new little boy cradled in her arms. Jenna and Josh were standing inside the front door, both smiling widely.

'Hi, guys. It's good to see you. You didn't stay away long.'

'No, I was keen to get back to the tea room. I felt a bit guilty leaving it with poor Ellie,' Jenna said, 'and Josh has got some big news. In fact, he's got three lots of big news.' Jenna turned and smiled at Josh, and Amelia thought how happy he looked.

'Hang on, I'll call Ben.'

'Don't worry, he's out at the shed. We saw him on the way in. He said he'll be in soon.'

Amelia frowned. She could swear she'd heard Ben talking outside.

'Guess what.' Jenna interrupted her thoughts. 'Josh has bought a property out on the Old Charleville Road.'

Amelia's eyes widened. 'You've bought a property? Here?'

Josh folded his arms and smiled at his sister. 'I am, Melie. Good enough for you to move here, sis? I thought I might come here too. There's a lot here to attract me.' He put his arm around Jenna's shoulders.

'Oh, that's wonderful news, Josh. I'm going to have some family here. And what are the other two bits of news?'

'Well, it's pretty special,' Josh said. 'It's like a bit of an early Christmas present for you.'

'Can I nurse Sebastian while you put your hands over your eyes?' Jenna asked with a wide smile.

'What is it? What have you brought back? Have you brought me something from home, or tell me you didn't bring me my horse, did you?'

'No, she wouldn't get in the plane.' Josh chuckled. 'It's a better surprise than that.'

'You've got me intrigued.'

Amelia handed Sebastian over to Jenna and smiled as she looked down at him with an envious look on her face.

'Now put your hands over your eyes,' Josh said, 'and don't peek. I have to go outside and get something.'

Amelia laughed. 'I guess I can do that.'

She did as she was told, and there was absolute silence in the room, apart from the door opening. After a minute or so, it closed again, and there was a rustling noise.

Josh came over and put his hand on her arm. 'Amelia, leave your hands on your eyes. Rightio, on the count of three, two, one. Okay you can look now.'

Amelia lowered her hands and looked at Josh. With a frown, her gaze moved to the left of him. Her eyes widened, and tears sprang to her eyes as she recognised the two women standing behind him.

'Mum?' Her voice squeaked. 'Oh my God, Mum, what are you doing here?' The tears rolled down her face as her mother stepped forward and put her arms around Amelia.

'Hello, darling. I've missed you so much.'

'Oh, Mummy, I've missed you too.' Amelia couldn't stop crying as her mother held her close, and it was a full minute before she reached out her hand to Molly. 'And Molly, you're here too. How long are you staying for?'

'Well, Dad and the boys are out mustering,' her mother replied. 'They bought some land up in the Gulf, and have a really big bush block up there now. So, they're out for a couple of weeks. Molly and I are going to stay till Boxing Day.'

'And where's Matt?' Amelia stepped out of her mother's arms and hugged her sister-in-law.

Molly's grin was wide. 'Matt's mustering with your dad and your brothers.'

Amelia's eyes were wide as her mother took her hand. 'We didn't tell you, but Dad had a bit of a turn about two months back, and he sat down and had a good long think after the muster. When I go back, he's going to leave the property in your brothers' charge and we're going away for a while.'

'Away?' Amelia frowned. 'Is he alright?'

'Yes, we're going to do a bit of travelling; we've bought a campervan and guess where the first stop is?'

'Augathella?' Amelia said tentatively.

'Spot on. I just came ahead to suss it out first,' she said, her smile teasing. 'Now let me hold my grandson.'

CHAPTER 9

Callie

It seemed that everyone in Augathella had decided to choose the second Sunday night in December for their Christmas party. The rural fire service had booked half the dining room, and the Country Women's Association were in the other half.

Braden and Callie Cartwright and their friends took up the street side of the bistro with three long tables joined together. In the middle of the bistro, there was a table for the children, and between those two tables, they left room to park four prams.

Braden grinned as he walked in. 'Looks like we've taken over the pub tonight, Callie.'

'Sure does,' she said, 'but how sad is it to walk in that door and not see Reg sitting there?

He would've loved this tonight, wouldn't he, Braden?'

'He would, but I think it's such a wonderful mark of respect that Sean and the staff have taken his table and chair away and put that pot plant under the plaque.'

Braden's eyes widened as he saw the tables. 'Holy heck, how many of us are here tonight?'

'Well, you think of everyone that we know and socialise with, and they're coming tonight. Saves a lot of individual visits. There wouldn't be enough nights before Christmas to catch up with everyone.'

'I'm pleased to see that Ruth and her husband are here too; it gives her a bit of a break. We'll make sure that she doesn't run after any of the kids tonight.'

'Yes, he came back from Brisbane,' she said. 'He's finished his contract there now, so she'll have someone in the house with her all the time.'

'But she's still going to babysit next year and she—'

'Yes, Fallon's got part-time work next year, and Ruth will have Ryan, the days that Fallon goes to work.'

'I'm behind on the times; the twins have kept us so busy.'

'They surely have,' Callie said, looking down at the two sleeping babies in the pram. They'd started sleeping a little better a couple of nights ago. 'They had a big feed before we left home, stayed awake in the car for most of the trip and now they're sound asleep.'

'Hopefully the noise won't bother them.'

'They need to get used to it.'

'I asked Sean specifically to arrange the tables like this so the kids could sit at the table behind us and be near the door. They can go out to the lawn and play after they eat. And we can put the prams in the middle here. If Amelia and

Ben, Sophie and Kent, Jon and Fallon, and you and I sit along here, we can just turn around and reach the prams. They won't be jammed in the corner.'

Braden put his arm across Callie's shoulders. 'You think of everything, Cal. What did I ever do without you?' He reached down and brushed a kiss on her cheek, and Callie smiled into her husband's eyes. Life couldn't get much better.

The only thing they hadn't done yet was talk to the boys about the trip to the Gold Coast. She and Braden had talked about it when they got home last night and decided to wait until after tonight.

Mind you, she thought, the boys had been closeted in Rory's room most of the day, and the hilarity hadn't been as loud as it had been the other day. *Maybe they'd lost interest in the project,* she wondered.

Sophie and Kent walked in, pushing the

pram.

'I'm so pleased you decided to come, Soph. It wouldn't have been the same without you.'

'Yeah, I couldn't miss Christmas at the pub,' she said.

'How's that little girl?'

'Perfect as usual. How are the twins?' Sophie asked hesitantly.

'Actually, sleeping a bit better,' Callie said.

'Look, here's Amelia and Ben,' Callie said as a third pram rolled into the bistro. She waited until they got closer and gestured to the space for the prams. 'This is the parking lot for the prams, guys. We can turn to the prams and the children easily without having to navigate the crowds.'

'That's fabulous,' Sophie said. 'Now let me have a look at this little boy of yours, Amelia.' She hadn't seen little Sebastian yet.

An olive-skinned face topped with jet-black hair beamed up at them, his dark eyes wide open.

'Oh my God, Amelia, he's absolutely gorgeous.'

Amelia looked up at Ben. 'We think so too.'

Ben smiled at his wife and then turned to Callie. 'We're only going to stay for a quick dinner because we had a wonderful surprise waiting when we got home at lunchtime today.'

'I heard you had some unexpected visitors.'

'Yes,' Amelia said with a laugh. 'Mum flew down from Granite Station, and Molly, my sister-in-law, came with Josh and Jenna from Darwin.'

'That's wonderful; you should've invited them tonight.'

'Jenna and Josh are coming, but Mum and Molly said they didn't want to impose on our Christmas night because they didn't know anybody.'

'They would've been most welcome,' Callie said.

'I know, but we'll just stay for dinner and then head back home. So good to see Mum, and she's absolutely smitten with Seb. Mum wanted to babysit, but he's due for a feed. So, if he has a feed, then goes to sleep, we might run him home and come back.'

'That sounds like a plan,' Callie said. A large group of people walked into the pub at the same time, and soon, the dining room was full, and their table was noisy as all their friends arrived and settled in. Callie glanced across at the children's table, where Rory and Nigel were in deep conversation. Petie was standing at the prams, moving from one to the other, looking at all the babies.

He wandered over to Callie, and she pulled him up to sit on her knee. 'You look very serious, Petie.'

'Mum, where do babies come from? And why did they all come at the same time? Was it like at a shop sale or something?'

Callie bit back her smile and hugged him close. 'That's something that we'll sit down and talk to you about in a while. All you need to know is that babies come when people love each other, but we all love you as much as we love our new babies.'

'But where do they come from?' Petie persisted.

'I think you need to talk to Daddy. Wait there.'

Petie nodded and waited.

'Braden,' Callie called over the noise. 'Petie needs to talk to you.'

CHAPTER 10

Callie

It was a fabulous night at the pub. Friendship, love, laughter and the satisfaction of perfectly-behaved twins enveloped Callie, as well as three well-behaved little boys. Sean had excelled himself getting the waitresses to decorate the Christmas tables for them. Gift-wrapped presents were exchanged, as the friends talked and laughed.

As they waited for dessert to be served, Callie sat back and reminisced about the last Christmas she spent in Brisbane. She had been alone in her house by the river, thinking of her family and feeling sad. Jen and the kids, along with her husband, Darren, had travelled north to Maryborough to celebrate Christmas with his family. Jen had always made sure that Callie was looked after during Christmas. They had been friends for a long time, and that particular Christmas had been very hard. Now, she looked around at her husband, her three beautiful stepsons, and her two adorable twins.

Fallon caught her eye across the table and smiled, and Callie could tell by the look on her face that her thoughts were taking a similar line.

Ruth had been the star of the show that night; she was such a lovely person. Everyone had looked after her very well, and she'd been a little bit tipsy.

Callie put a hand over her mouth and smiled as Ruth looked at her. 'No more drinks. Ben wants to buy me a dessert wine.'

'You deserve to have a good night, Ruth. Enjoy yourself,' Callie added, winking at her.

The only thing that Callie hadn't been sure about that night was the three boys. Even though they had behaved well and eaten their meal without complaint—even vegetables with their baked dinner—Nigel and Rory had been subdued. Each time Callie looked over, they were writing on a piece of paper and seemed to be crossing off items. Every so often, they both got up and walked to each end of the table to talk to the adults.

She was proud of them. It was lovely of them to make sure they wished everybody a Merry Christmas. At one point, Nigel walked past, and she grabbed his hand. 'Are you having a good time?'

'I am, Mum. Thank you. Have to go. Rory's got a job for me.'

She wondered what they were up to, but whatever it was, they were behaving, and they weren't fighting. Petie spent most of his time at the four prams, looking at the babies quietly and smiling at her every time she caught his eye. Braden had fobbed him off with a promise to talk tomorrow. Callie sat back, a wave of contentment and love filling her.

The night was in full swing when Rory came up to her and asked if he could say a few words to everyone.

'I think that's okay. What do you want to say?'

'It's alright. I just want to say Merry Christmas and thank you to everybody.'

She put her arm around his waist, and he snuggled into her.

'That's lovely, Rory. Dad and I are really proud of you boys tonight. You've all been so well-behaved.'

Rory grinned, and she wondered about the look on his face. 'Nigel is going to talk with me too.'

'Braden, can you get the attention of the table? The two boys want to say something.'

Petie turned her face. 'Me too.'

Callie and Braden looked at each other, and

Braden shrugged. He stood and tapped his dessert spoon on his beer glass.

'Can I have your attention, please, everyone?'

It took a couple of minutes, but eventually, there was silence.

'First of all, I want to say thanks, everyone, for coming tonight. What a great night we're having, and I hope you all have a Merry Christmas. Got a couple of boys here who wanted to say Merry Christmas as well.'

There was a little round of applause. Nigel stood beside the table next to Braden. Rory stood straight with his shoulders back, and then Nigel moved behind him with a wide grin on his face.

'Thank you, Dad.' Rory looked over and saw Petie over by the prams. 'Nigel and Petie and I want to say Merry "Christmas to everybody too.'

A chorus of "Merry Christmas, boys" filled the room. 'Hope Santa brings you everything you want.'

'Thank you,' Rory said. 'We also want to wish Mum and Dad a happy Christmas.'

Callie blinked back a tear.

'But most of all, we want to thank everyone we've spoken to tonight for letting us use them.'

Callie frowned. 'Use them?'

'We just have to finish it off tomorrow before we go to school and hand it in. Then on Friday, we'll know if we've won.'

There was a big round of applause, and Callie and Braden looked at each other. 'What are they talking about?' Braden asked.

'I don't know,' Callie said. 'But they're up to something with that play.' She shrugged. 'No one seems upset about it, so we can ask them when we get home.'

'Good luck with that,' Braden said. 'If Rory and Nigel decide to keep a secret, you can't pry it from them. Not even with torture,' he said with a grin.

'Don't be like that.'

'You'll see.'

Dessert was a flaming Bombe Alaska for the tables. Sean had excelled himself, and the children's eyes were wide as a miniature version was put on their table and then the flames extinguished. Petie leaned over to Callie. 'Can I just have ice cream, please, Mum?'

'You can have whatever you want, sweetie.'

The night came to an end, and there was much hugging and wishing of Merry Christmas as Christmas paper, wrapped gifts, and bon bon scraps were put in the bin. Rory, Nigel's and Petie's presents remained wrapped on the table.

'Do you want to open your presents, boys?'

'No, we're going put them under the Christmas tree,' Rory said.

'You're growing up fast,' she said, giving him a quick hug before she stood and went over to the pram; the twins were still sound asleep. 'What's the chances of you staying asleep till we get home for a feed?' she asked aloud.

'They'll be good. They'll learn off their big brothers how to behave,' Braden said.

'I'm sure they will. Come on, family, it's time we hit the road.' Braden put his arm around Callie's shoulders as they pushed the pram together towards the door, and their three boys forged ahead.

A few minutes later they were out of the township and headed along the dirt road to Kilcoy Station.

Callie smiled at Braden. Nigel and Rory were talking quietly in the backseat, and she turned around to check on them. Petie was already asleep. She turned back to the front and put her hand on Braden's thigh. 'That was nice of the boys to wish everyone a Merry Christmas,' she said.

'It was.' Braden raised his voice a bit. 'Tell us a little bit more about your play, boys. You were talking about using some of our friends in the play, weren't you? When you wished everyone Merry Christmas. That was a good thing to do. I was proud of you.'

Callie waited for the reply from the back, but it didn't come.

'Yeah, the play's going well,' Rory said finally.

Braden looked at Callie and raised his eyebrows.

'Can you tell us what it's about?' Callie asked.

'It's a nativity play about joy, happiness, and Christmas, and it's got a donkey in it,' Rory replied.

'A special donkey?' Callie inquired.

She looked over the back, and he said, 'No, just an ordinary donkey.' His face was a picture of innocence.

'The winner's going to be announced this week, is that right?' she asked.

'Yes, it is. At Presentation Assembly,' Nigel said. 'I reckon we're going to win.'

Braden frowned and glanced across at Callie.

'Boys, we have something to tell you.' Braden's voice was loud enough for the boys to hear, but not enough to wake the twins. 'We're going to go down to the Gold Coast and visit Dreamworld and SeaWorld and Movie World.'

'Yay!' both boys yelled together.

Callie turned in her seat and looked over into the back seat. 'There's only one problem. If we go to the Gold Coast before Christmas, we won't be here for the Christmas play.'

Nigel's mouth dropped open as he put his hands on the back of Braden's seat, his eyes wide. 'Not gonna happen.'

'You mean you don't want to go away and do all those fun things?' Callie asked.

'No, we don't want to,' Rory replied. 'Not if it means missing the play. Mum, we've worked so hard on our story.'

'What if your play doesn't get chosen? Would you be happy to go away then?' Callie questioned.

Nigel shook his head quickly from side to side. 'That's not going to happen, either. We're going to win.'

'So, you wouldn't mind missing out on the theme parks so you can produce your play?'

'Yes, we want to do it. We can go to Dreamworld and those places any old time, can't we?'

Braden shrugged and Callie stared at him.

'So, when do we find out who the winning entry belongs to?'

'This Friday, Dad. And really, even if we

113

don't win, I think it's poor form if we leave the school and don't see whoever's play wins, that is. It might look like we're bad losers. You know what I mean. If we don't win then we leave town. That's pretty rude, you know.'

Braden frowned and met Callie's eyes.

'We don't have to worry about that, Rory. We're going to win,' Nigel repeated.

All was quiet for a while as the vehicle headed along the dirt road towards home.

Finally, Braden spoke quietly. 'I think we may have to reconsider our trip. What do you think, Cal?'

'Sounds like it. I hate to think that the boys would be considered sore losers if we leave town. We know they're not, but they don't want others to get the wrong idea.'

'Okay, I won't book the apartment till Friday,' Braden said. 'I'll email them and say that we've had a change of plans. You disappointed?'

'To tell the truth,' Callie said hesitantly, 'not really. I was dreading packing up the babies and all the assorted paraphernalia in the Land Cruiser. Maybe in the June school holidays when it's cooler out here, we can pack up and take them down to Brisbane and stay at my house. We can do day trips to the Gold Coast. How does that sound?'

'Whatever suits you best, my love.'

Callie pulled a face at him. 'You didn't want to go away either, did you?'

CHAPTER 11

Emily

Between assessments, reports, and Christmas preparations, as well as teaching her class in the daytime, Emily's three-day school week flew by. It was Wednesday night after she had put Ophelia down before she got a chance to read the seventeen Christmas play entries.

Kimberley had been overwhelmed by the response to the literacy competition, and the whole school, staff and students, had been talking about it. Not to mention the number of parents who mentioned it as they picked up their children at the school. Excitement was buzzing about Augathella Primary School's Christmas play.

Rory and Nigel Cartwright had tagged behind her when she did playground duty a couple of days this week and tried to engage her in conversation about when she was going to read them. But Emily didn't let on that she hadn't started. She smiled and nodded. 'Yes, boys, going well.'

As she sat at the small desk in her room that night, she looked over at the cot. Her daughter was sound asleep; Ophelia had been sleeping well since she'd been spending her days at Ruth's. Even though Emily had the next two days at home to read the plays, she decided to complete them tonight. Christmas shopping in Charleville was a possibility for tomorrow. She wanted to get some gifts for the staff at school, and now that she had a regular salary, she was in a position to spend some money. Plus, she needed some Santa presents for Ophelia and something for Jenna. She wanted to get a very special gift for Ruth. Although she paid Ruth to look after Ophelia, Ruth's care of her little girl went above and beyond the money she would accept. She was a wonderful woman, and Ophelia adored her.

Some of the plays had been typed up and printed out, and Emily wondered, maybe unfairly, how many parents had actually helped the students with the project. She was sure she'd be able to pick it up by the language and the setting out. She flicked through the papers until she came across the one from the Cartwright boys.

Their entry was handwritten in pencil, and some of the pages had what looked like food stains and dirty fingerprints on them. Emily smiled; one crinkled page looked like it had been screwed up and then flattened. Plus, there were some drawings and diagrams on the back of the paper that looked like genuine works in progress. She laughed as she saw the rough drawing of a donkey costume and a cushion.

She put their entry at the bottom of the pile; the boys were so keen she should see what the competition was like before she got to that one. But no favourites.

Emily pulled out her marking criteria and sat it on the desk beside her pencil.

Out of the entries she read in the first half hour, it was disappointing that some children had obviously been assisted by parents.

The next five entries were obviously the work of the students, but they did not meet the criteria for theme. There was no mention of the nativity scene, no Mary and Joseph in several. It was mainly about Santa Claus coming to Augathella, going down chimneys with assorted presents, with a bit of "Christmas brings joy to everyone" at the end. She did smile, however, when in one story Santa did manage to get a donkey down the chimney.

The three entries she read after that were

possibilities, and she put them aside. With a bit of work and creativity, they could be turned into a play. That was something she would have to work on over the weekend once she decided on the winning entry. When it was announced, she could work with the student or group that created it.

Finally, Emily reached the stained and crumpled entry of the Cartwright boys and suppressed a smile. The entry was just like the boys—full of passion, enthusiasm, and creativity. She switched the desk lamp on before she started and then decided to go make a cup of tea before she read the last entry.

She headed out to the kitchen; Jenna and Joshua were out for dinner for the night, and it was almost as if she had an apartment to herself. It would be nice to have her own place, especially if the work next year came through as Bob had said.

Her gut told her it was a certainty, but until she signed on the bottom line, Emily wasn't sure. She also needed to sort out Luke on Sunday night when they went out for dinner, to tell him that if she did stay in town next year, he would have to realise they were just friends and for him to give up the foolish hope that they could rekindle their relationship of years ago.

Not that it needed rekindling. Emily knew she had never stopped loving Luke Elliott.

She reached up to get a chamomile tea bag out of the caddy and then stood at the kitchen window as she waited for the kettle to boil. The sun had long set, and darkness had stolen over the back garden. For the first time in a long time, Emily felt content and secure. She was starting to make some good friends, and she loved the children at the school. Jenna was the best landlady that she could ask for, and Ruth was almost like a grandmother to her daughter, and in a way, a surrogate mother to Emily.

Ruth always engaged her in conversation at the end of each day when Emily picked up Ophelia, wanting to know how her day was, what she was planning for dinner, and always giving her some sort of treat—a small container of biscuits, a slice of homemade cake or some fresh fruit that she'd bought at the supermarket.

'You spoil me, Ruth.'

'You deserve spoiling, Emily. I worry about you.'

'There's no need. I'm used to looking after myself.'

Ruth had looked at her intently. One day, Emily thought she would share her story with the older woman. Troy's suicide had traumatised her, and she could recognise that. Maybe one day she'd get past it, maybe one day she'd have confidence in herself to have a relationship.

As she poured the hot water over the

chamomile, surprise stole over her. For the first time, she had started to think positively in terms of healing. She wouldn't tell Luke what she was thinking; he might get his hopes up high.

Reaching for one of the peanut butter biscuits Ruth had packed in a plastic container for her to bring home today, Emily put it on the saucer and headed back to her room.

Ophelia had kicked the sheets off, and Emily pulled them halfway up over her. It was too hot to be completely covered up tonight. Maybe when they went to Charleville, she'd find a fan to put in their room.

Her daughter lay on her back, her face set in a contented pose. Her dark lashes framed her rosy cheeks, and her tiny fingers were curled up in fists resting on her tummy. A wave of love so strong it almost hurt ran through Emily, and tears filled her eyes.

'Troy, oh Troy, couldn't you see what we

could have had?'

Her grief counsellor in Cairns had told her that Troy would have felt that suicide was the only way to end an unbearable pain he was feeling as the result of trauma in his life and it could have come from many years ago.

Emily had shaken her head. 'I don't know what it would have been. I need to understand why.'

'Emily? You need to understand you may never know. When you accept that, your healing will start.'

She had known that Troy hadn't been in a good place for a long time, and she had to accept that and move on. It wasn't healthy for her to dwell on the whys when she had no chance of discovering the cause. She had tried to talk to his mother and had had no success.

Emily sighed, put the teacup and saucer on the desk and switched on the lamp above the computer as she settled down to read. Halfway through the play penned by Nigel and Rory Cartwright, she was laughing out loud.

It was balm for her soul. She was laughing so much she almost choked on a crumb of a peanut butter cookie, and she had to put the teacup down so she didn't sputter tea all over the already stained play.

This was the winning entry; there was absolutely no doubt, she knew by the time she reached the end. Her laughter had turned into tears, and she marvelled at the insight those three boys had. She knew they had suffered tragedy; they had lost their mother, and then their Aunt Sophie had cared for them for eighteen months as Braden had dealt with his grief.

Braden had married Callie almost a year after she had come west from Brisbane to be a nanny to the boys. That scene in the play had made Emily laugh and cry; it gave her a whole new picture of Braden and Callie.

Callie had not hesitated to tell Emily her story. Now they had their twins, and they were so happy together. The amount of love that these boys were obviously given showed through in every word they wrote, and Emily sat back, tears rolling down her face.

They understood the power of love at eight and ten. How could she not understand it at twenty-nine? Emily pushed the play to the side of the desk, put her hands over her face, and began to sob.

CHAPTER 12

Callie

Callie attended the school assembly on Friday. She didn't work Fridays, and neither did Emily but she knew Emily would come in to announce the winners of the play. The boys had driven her and Braden crazy all week— breakfast, dinner, bedtime, first thing in the morning, and feeding the animals. The topic of conversation had been the play, who was going to be in it, how they were going to produce it, and what props they would need.

Callie was going to Charleville to shop on Saturday and the boys had extracted a promise that they could come too. There was a bargain store in town that had everything they could possibly need. However, Callie had to promise that they could shop by themselves as everything was to be a surprise.

'You have to win yet,' she reminded them after dinner on Thursday as they made a secret shopping list.

'We'll win,' they both said together.

Later that night when the three boys were in bed, Callie sat in the living room beside Braden as he flicked through Netflix.

'You do realise they are going to be devastated if they don't win this competition.'

Braden frowned, 'Yeah, I know. And to top it all off, they'll have to watch someone else's play performed, and we won't be going down to the coast. Maybe we could go after Christmas if they're miserable.'

'Well, let's not jump to conclusions. You never know; they've put so much work into it, maybe they'll win.'

'With a farting donkey?' Braden said, 'I don't think they've got a hope in hell, sweetheart.'

Now Callie pushed the double pram into the assembly hall. There were four rows of chairs for parents at the back, and she took a seat in the back row so there was room for the double pram beside her. Petie sat in the chair on the other side, and she wondered how he'd last for the full hour. Meggie and Munro had had a broken night and were now sound asleep.

'That'd be right,' she thought as she covered a yawn.

There was still the grocery shopping to do after the hour here. If the twins behaved, she'd call into Jenna's and have a cup of coffee at the Vintage Tearoom, and feed the babies before she headed for the grocery store.

It was a long assembly today because it was the day when the children received their class awards.

Emily walked down the space between the

two groups of children, in the centre of the hall, and sat with the staff at the side of the stage.

Bob Hamblin stood at the lectern on the stage and welcomed the parents. The next half hour was filled with two performances by students from prep and grade four, and then the school choir singing Christmas carols with Kimberley conducting. Craig Anderson's son recited a Christmas poem.

Callie's eyes got heavier and she had to force herself to stay awake. It was hot in the hall, despite the large fans circulating air overhead. Meggie began to stir and she reached into the pram and gently patted her back.

Finally, the certificates were presented to each year from prep to grade six. Meggie settled and Callie leaned back in the chair and closed her eyes. After a minute or two, she forced herself to wake up as they got to Nigel's class. She sat up straight, clapping as he was presented with his certificate and a merit award for being a good class monitor.

Finally, it was Rory's turn, and he received a merit certificate for his work in mathematics, his improvement in writing, and his knowledge of geography. She cheered and clapped, full of pride. A full fifty-five minutes had passed since she'd sat down, and she glanced into the pram, the twins were still sound asleep. Knowing her luck, they would wake up for a feed soon, and she'd miss the contest announcement.

Ruth had said to drop them in any time she wanted to, but Callie relied on her too much. She'd have to learn how to cope.

Relief shot through her as the twins slept on, and Petie sat quietly taking it all in as Bob called Emily to the stage.

'Now, I'm going ask Mrs Jansen to come to the stage and announce the winner of our Christmas play competition.' The principal beamed. 'Congratulations to all who managed to write a play. That's a big achievement. Mrs Jansen tells me that they were all great stories, but of course, there's only one winner. We're looking forward to starting rehearsals next week, and this play will be performed on Saturday of next weekend here in the primary school hall. I'm sure you'll all be here, and boys and girls, someone told me that there might be a visit from a man in a red suit after the play's over.' As Emily made her way to the stage, the children clapped and cheered at the thought of Santa Claus coming to the primary school.

Callie sat there; her fingers crossed. She could see Rory's head in the group of children, and Nigel was a monitor so he was standing at the side.

Emily took the microphone. 'Thank you, Mr. Hamblin. I must say it's been an absolute pleasure reading all your stories, but we have a winning entry, and I'm looking forward to talking with the authors this afternoon and taking them through the script I've written from their story. The winner of the Christmas literacy competition and the authors'— Callie's heart gave a little skip at the plural—'the authors of this play have done a fine job.'

Emily nodded slowly. 'Not only did they capture the spirit of Christmas and the theme of love and joy with the Christmas story in a contemporary setting, they made me laugh, and I must admit, they made me cry.'

Callie's hopes sank; she couldn't imagine a story with a farting donkey would make anyone cry, unless it was with tears of laughter.

'Now, I would like to ask the winners of our competition to come to the stage so Mr Hamblin can give them a special certificate for winning the Christmas play competition.'

Callie held her breath as Emily looked out

over the children. Bob Hamblin took the microphone from her and made a drumroll sound while Emily waited.

Emily hesitated as she waited for the microphone, and Callie's heart raced.

'Gosh, what must the boys be going through?' she wondered. She glanced across at Nigel and saw the instant his expression changed.

Emily smiled. 'Rory and Nigel Cartwright, please come up and receive your certificates.'

The hall erupted in an uproar of yells and screams, clapping and cheering. Callie blinked back tears as Nigel and Rory made their way to the stage. Petie leaned over with a big grin. 'See, I knew they'd win, Mum.'

Braden was waiting at home to hear. Callie pulled out her phone and sent a text:

They won!!!!!!!!!!!!

CHAPTER 13

Luke

Strong crosswinds buffeted Luke's plane as he brought it to a quick landing at the Augathella aerodrome. He'd had every intention of getting back to town early and having a leisurely shower while planning what he was going to say to Emily over dinner tonight.

As he taxied the aircraft and then came to a stop near the hangar, he looked at his watch. By the time he secured the aircraft, and called a taxi to take him back into town—because he wasn't going to walk the distance from the aerodrome this afternoon like he usually did—he'd barely have enough time to have a shower and head down to Emily's to pick her up at six o'clock.

It was all Braden Cartwright's fault; Kent Mason had come over from his place, and they spent a couple of hours yakking about plans for next year. Luke had lost track of time until he looked at his watch and saw how late it was.

'Gotta go, guys. I've got a date.'

Braden grinned. 'Let me guess, Emily Jansen?'

Luke nodded and smiled. 'Send me positive vibes and wish me luck tonight; I'm trying to make a breakthrough.'

The taxi arrived quickly, and Bert, the driver of the only taxi in town, looked at Luke when he said he was going to the pub.

'You could've walked there, mate.'

'Yeah, I know, but I'm in a rush,' Luke said. He paid the fare, raced up the steps to his room, jumped in the shower, and stood there, trying to catch his breath as he planned what he was going to say to Emily.

He knew deep down that she cared about him, and he had no doubt that he loved her. He was going to tell her that tonight, and if she wasn't interested, well, he wouldn't come back to Augathella after Christmas. He was committed here until Christmas Eve, and then he was due back in Narrabri.

He had a month of leave then, and he had to figure out what he was going to do. If Emily stayed here next year—and she said that she was going to be offered work—with any luck, he wouldn't come back here. It was time to spread his wings, literally and figuratively and travel more widely with his job. If Dwyer Holdings weren't prepared to let him go to Western Australia to work, he could resign and do contract work. He had the reputation that would get him work. It all hinged on Emily tonight. Luke had decided that he was going to be totally honest, even if she didn't want to talk. He was going to force her to. It might be cruel, but it was the only way they could come to some sort of understanding. He jumped out of the shower, quickly dried off, and then ran a razor over his face to make sure it was clean-shaven, just in case.

***

Emily got ready in a daze; she knew she wanted to look her best. But she stood at her wardrobe for a good two minutes, trying to choose between the black dress or the floral dress she bought in Charleville when she went down to buy Christmas presents for Ophelia last week. The floral dress won out because it was a close match to her sandals, and once she was out of the shower, she slipped it over her head.

Ophelia was sitting on the living room floor, playing with those beloved blocks. She had bought a new set for Christmas, but she wondered if she'd wasted her money because Ophelia loved the brightly-coloured set they had had for the last six months. She picked them up and began stacking blocks.

Her hand shook as she tried to apply her makeup. She was terrified of talking to Luke tonight, but that's what she was going to do; it was time for honesty. Those two little boys, the Cartwrights, would never have any idea of what they'd done for her, how she saw the error of her ways. She realised that the path she'd been on was not the right one.

She'd always loved Luke Elliott, and she knew that he cared about her. What had happened was in the past, and the examples that those two little boys had given, and how they related it to happiness in the town, had opened her eyes. It was time that she moved on. She couldn't carry that burden for the rest of her life because it would taint Ophelia's upbringing. She needed to look at the positives and think about what was the best for both of them, what was the best for the three of them.

'Hello, Emily.'

'Hello, Luke,' she said. She stood at the door, her fingers gripping the door handle. Jen and Joshua were still out, and she'd had the house to herself. Ophelia was sitting in the pram, gripping her little ragdoll, and she smiled when she spotted Luke at the door.

'Hello, Ophelia. How's the prettiest girl in the world today?'

Emily tipped her head to the side and put on a coquettish smile. 'The prettiest girl in the world?'

'After her mother, of course,' Luke said with a smile.

It was going to be alright. Emily knew it was going to be alright. She locked the doors, and Luke manoeuvred the stroller down the steps.

It was a lovely evening. The wind from earlier had dropped, a gentle breeze blowing, keeping it cool. Jenna's front garden was a riot of colours—petunias, lobelia, and geraniums spilled out over the garden edge. The fragrance of the single rose she had growing in a pot next to the gate drifted on the evening air.

Emily opened the gate as Luke pushed the stroller out, and she swallowed. She followed him. Luke kept the stroller on the grass of the footpath as they headed towards the pub, and Emily walked beside them. Neither of them spoke. It appeared that Luke was lost in his thoughts as much as she was.

She swallowed again. 'Luke,' she asked quietly.

'Yes, Em?'

'Would it be okay if I held your hand as we walk to the pub?'

The smile that broke over his face filled her with joy, the same joy that the boys had written about in their play.

'It sure would.' He held out his hand, and

Emily laced her fingers through his, and their eyes met. It was going to be alright.

Ophelia sat happily in the high chair the bistro provided.

'Would you like a drink, Emily?' Luke asked.

'I would, please. I'll have a glass of bubbles.'

Luke raised his eyebrows. A lump stuck in his throat as he thought about the talk he wanted to have over dinner. Was he doing the right thing?

'Yes.' His conscience nagged at him. They had to talk. He had to know whether he was wasting his time. Emily asking if she could hold his hand on the way to the pub had filled him with hope, but he didn't want to get his hopes up too much.

He came back to the table with two glasses

of champagne and put them in front of his place. 'I feel as though we should be toasting a celebration.'

'We should be, shouldn't we?' Emily held his gaze, her heart starting to beat faster.

'Did you want to order yet? Or just sit and have a drink for a while?'

'Let's have a drink and chat before we order,' she said.

'Thank you for coming out with me tonight, Emily. I really appreciate it.'

'My pleasure,' she said. 'Thank you for inviting me.' Every time he looked at her, he saw her eyes on him, and Luke's hopes began to build even more. So, he decided to take the plunge.

'Emily, I hope it doesn't upset you, but I really want to talk tonight.'

'So do I, Luke. What did you want to talk about?' Her eyes snagged his and held them.

'I want to talk about Troy,' she said.

Luke had to consciously stop his mouth from dropping open.

'Yes, the elephant that's in the room between us, the one that I refused to talk about.'

'You want to talk about Troy?'

'I realise that I've been wrong, Luke. I've been wrong for three years. I'll never regret it because I have my beautiful little girl from that relationship. I had decided that it was my fault, that I was responsible for what he did. But something happened this week that made me think deeply and long and hard, and I know it wasn't me. Troy had issues, and we hadn't really been a couple since the first year we were married.'

Luke reached over and took her hand, and her fingers brushed his. 'It was never your fault, Emily. Troy has always carried his demons. You know what caused it, don't you?'

He was surprised when Emily shook her

head. 'No, I have no idea. I just knew he had black moods. At first, I blamed myself, and then I realised it wasn't me.'

'You don't know what happened?' Luke said.

'No,' she said again.

'Did you know about his father?'

'No, I just know that his mother lives in America with her second husband.'

'How old were you when you came to Narrabri High?'

'We moved there when I was in Year Eight.'

'Yes, I couldn't remember what year it was.'

'Why do you ask?'

'Because when we were in Year Seven . . .' Luke paused. Her eyes were holding his, and they were wide. 'When we were in Year Seven, Troy discovered his father had been embezzling money from his work account, and rather than face investigation, he killed himself.'

'I never knew that,' Emily said.

'The worst part is that Troy found him; his father hung himself in the garage.'

Emily's eyes filled with tears, and Luke wondered if he had gone too far in telling her.

'You didn't ever know?'

'No, I didn't. He would never talk about anything in the past.'

'I can understand that. He had a terrible childhood. He was pretty much left to do his own thing, and when his father killed himself, his mother fled. She left Troy with a neighbour to finish off his Year Seven, and then, by the time you came to town, care was finalised for him. He moved in with his aunt and uncle.'

'That's right; they never told me what it was like either. I had to make the call to tell them when he crashed the helicopter.'

Luke's fingers grasped his glass. 'I'm sorry, Emily. I should've told you when I could see you falling for Troy. I thought you'd be good for him, but I upset that you'd moved on.'

'I was never good for him; Troy never loved me. I don't know why he married me.'

But she reached over with her other hand and touched her fingers to his cheek. 'Maybe he knew that I needed something, and look, I've got a beautiful little girl.'

'You've just got to look at Ophelia and remember that she's a good part of Troy.'

'She is; she does look a little bit like him, but you know Troy was never interested in her.'

'He didn't have much confidence, Emily; I don't think he had any idea of how to have a relationship after his father died. I was stunned when he started asking you out. You know why he did, don't you?'

'I do. Because he was jealous of you, and that I was starting to care about you. We were good mates, Luke, good friends. I've had an experience this week that has taught me to be honest, so I will be. If it means you get in your plane and leave tomorrow, I'll still be honest. I'm sorry for the way I've treated you over the past couple of weeks, and that I didn't tell you how many times I thought of you after we left Narrabri to go north. I missed you every day, and I knew I'd made a mistake, but I was going to commit to my promise. To the wedding vows I made. But it just got harder and harder, and then when he died, I just shut down. I blamed myself, and I tried to push you out of my thoughts. When I saw you in Augathella, I couldn't believe it, and it all came rushing back, and I knew I was in trouble. That's why I fought so hard.'

Emotion flowed through Luke, and his eyes pricked with emotion. 'Emily, I can't believe what you just said. You've made me the happiest man in the world tonight. I was going to be honest too. If you just wanted to be my friend, I was going to let you have your year here and fly somewhere else and leave you in peace.'

Emily's eyes opened wide, and she held his. 'I love you, Luke Elliott. I always have, and I know I always will.'

'And I love you, Emily and I love your little girl. Can you see a future with me?'

Emily's eyes filled with tears as she looked at him. 'I can.'

CHAPTER 14

Callie and Braden

The Play:

Love and Joy come to Augathella

Written by Rory and Nigel Cartwright

There was standing room only in the hall at Augathella Primary School half an hour before the Christmas play was due to begin. Luke was on chair duty and he'd called to Kent to help as the carpark filled and the queue outside the hall lengthened.

Emily and Kimberley Riordan were standing at the front door selling tickets.

'We can't let any more in,' Bob Hamblin said as he hurried past. 'It would be a fire hazard.' He stopped when he spotted Braden and Callie waiting at the door with Sophie and Petie.

Nigel and Rory were already backstage.

'Welcome, Braden and Callie,' he said. 'There are three reserved seats for you at the front, for you and Mr. Mason.'

'What about Petie and Sophie?' Callie frowned.

Bob tapped a finger on the side of his nose. 'They don't need seats. They have some special duties.'

Callie turned to look at Sophie. 'You've got a special duty?'

Sophie nodded. 'I sure do. You'll see. So does Ruby Rose.'

Callie turned to Petie but he'd already gone. Sophie grinned up at Kent. 'Enjoy the show.'

Callie shook her head as Sophie took off after Petie pushing the pram.

It had been a week of secrets. She'd taken the three boys to Charleville on Saturday after they heard they'd won and she waited with the twins in the coffee shop next door while they did their shopping. Rory looked very grown-up when Callie handed over her credit card and told him the PIN.

'Mum,' he said, 'you're not allowed to look at your online bank stuff until after the play. You're not allowed to know what we've bought, okay? Do you promise?' he said.

'Yes, I promise.' Callie was intrigued. They had carried out two big parcels wrapped in brown paper, and had asked to drop them off at the school on the way home.

'Mrs Jansen will be there, and we're going to rehearse.'

'Have you picked all the cast already?' Callie tried for some information with no luck.

'You'll see. Dad can come back in and pick us up later.'

'Okay.'

Rehearsals had been on all week. The

children involved had been pulled from class—apparently Rory and Nigel had already chosen them at the writing stage—and rehearsals filled the day. Callie had worked on Monday, and had been banned from the hall. When she'd walked past a couple of times, all she could hear was laughter.

The twins were with Ruth who'd called and insisted, 'You won't be able to focus on the play if the twins wake up.'

'But you should see it too,' Callie had insisted.

'No, I'll see the video.'

'The video? Callie asked.

'Yes, Jon is filming it. It's one of the hobbies I didn't know my son-in-law had.'

'Talk about a production and a half,' Callie said to Braden when she took his cup of tea out to the shed, halfway through the week. 'The play's being filmed.'

Braden nodded absently. 'What did you need your red suitcases for? Did you get them out before we decided not to go away?'

Callie stared at him. 'I haven't touched them. Why?'

'I was looking for my kit bag to take mustering next week, and they're not there. I wondered how you'd reached them up there.'

'I have no idea where they are. I haven't had them out since you put them there after they dried.'

'That was a long time ago.' Braden leaned over and kissed her. 'That's one of my best memories of when we met.'

'I'm not a city slicker any more. I'd know not to hide luggage in an irrigation channel these days, plus I know a lot more than that.'

'You sure do. Anyway, they'll turn up.'

Callie didn't give them another though until Emily stood at the front and the play began.

She tapped the microphone that was on the stand in front of the closed curtains. 'Welcome everyone, parents, children, family and friends. We have a special presentation tonight. Also, after the play has finished, there is a special supper being served in the quadrangle, jointly catered for by Jenna's Vintage Tearooms and the CWA. If you'd like to purchase a cuppa and cake, all proceeds are going to our branch of the rural fire service.'

The audience applauded.

Emily continued. 'If you think back to the 1920s when films were all action with dialogue unspoken, you will understand the gist of the Cartwright brothers' play. I think we can look forward to seeing playwrights or filmmakers of the future.'

'Like Smiley Creevey,' someone called from the front.

Emily nodded. 'So, this evening, I am going

to be the narrator, and the action will unfold in front of you.' She smiled. 'We need you to know that no children, babies or animals will be harmed in this production.'

'Thank goodness for that,' Braden whispered as he reached over and squeezed Callie's hand. Pride emanated from him as he stared ahead.

'I give you, *Love and Joy come to Augathella,*' Emily said to thunderous applause.

'And now to begin.' As Emily spoke the lights dimmed and the curtains opened.

A contemporary play. Callie smiled. One criterion ticked off.

Two children sat on the stage beside a manger, and it was clear that they had to be Joseph and Mary, although they were dressed in jeans and T-shirts.

'It took Joseph and Mary a long time to reach Bethlehem. It was like a trip travelling from

Brisbane to Augathella.'

Callie and Braden smiled at each other. She knew that trip well.

'When they arrived, Mary was very tired. They needed to find somewhere to stay, but the town was crowded with lots of people and every motel was full. A kind pub owner took pity on them and let them stay in his stable down the back.'

Callie frowned as a young girl dressed in red walked onto the stage carrying her two red suitcases.

'My suitcases, Braden,' she hissed. 'That's my suitcases!'

'And look to the left,' he said. 'A cardboard cutout red sports car. I'm nervous,' he said.

'Hmm,' Callie said as Emily began to speak again.

'And now we move to the love and joy in our town. Once upon a time, a lonely man with three

157

little boys rescued a damsel in distress.'

Braden chuckled along with the rest of the audience.

'And the power of love—and water—' Emily paused. A collective gasp sounded from the audience as a bucket of water was tipped over the girl in red from above. Her hair was stuck to her face, and she turned as a grade six boy walked onto the stage followed by three boys from the prep class. He kneeled in front of the young girl, and his hands went into a beseeching position in front of his chest.

'The power of love,' Emily continued, 'ensured that true love followed its course. resulting in joy for a very sad family in the town of Augathella.'

The girl nodded and took the boy's hand and they exited the stage on the left side with the three small boys skipping happily after them.

Callie looked at Braden as tears rolled down

her cheeks. 'That's us and the boys.'

Braden's mouth was set straight and she could swear a tear glinted in his eyes. 'It is.'

Before they could think about that scene, a donkey shuffled onto the stage. Callie leaned over to Braden and whispered. 'That's Nigel and Rory, I recognise their shoes.'

Emily continued. 'During the night Mary gave birth to Jesus. She put him in his baby clothes and laid him in a manger full of hay.'

As they watched the curtain at the back of the set moved and a hand appeared. It reached down and a short baby cry came from the manger.

'A huge thank you to our youngest star, Ruby Rose Mason, who is playing Baby Jesus in the manger,' Emily continued with a wide smile. Callie gasped as Sophie poked her head through the curtains and smiled.

The donkey turned and ambled out, it paused

near the exit and a loud noise emitted from the side of the stage.

Braden cackled out loud. 'Oh, Cal, they were allowed to have the farting donkey.'

'Were they?' she asked, wiping tears of mirth from her eyes. 'Or was that unscripted?'

The answer came as Emily returned to the microphone. 'A special thank you to Petie Cartwright for the sounds effects, courtesy of a whoopee cushion, sponsored by the Charleville Bargain Store.'

Emily looked to the right of the stage as a boy ran in holding a large plastic helicopter.

'Soon, the power of love and wind'— Emily smiled— 'at this point I may need to remind you that wind also powers helicopters before there is further need of sound effects . . . yet.'

By this stage everyone in the hall was laughing and smiling.

'Again, the power of love,' Emily continued,

'ensured that true love followed its course. resulting in joy for a lonely pair in the town of Augathella.'

Ben and Amelia were next, with a special appearance by Chilli Girl on stage.

Braden whispered, 'I can see where that reminder of "no babies or animals being harmed" came from!'

The donkey reappeared from the side, crossed the stage and the same sound effect brought the house down.

'Look at that pair of rascals, Cal, they're laughing so much, the costume is going to slip off if they're not careful.'

Callie let out a sigh of relief as the donkey left the stage. 'Hopefully no-one else will know it's our boys.'

Braden's eyes met hers and he smiled. 'I love you,' he mouthed. 'Here's the next scene.' They laughed as a doctor ran across the stage to sit beside a demure young lady who had sat on a picnic rug.

'How did they know all this!' Callie exclaimed. 'That's Dr Harry and Laura!'

'Your boys don't miss a trick,' Kent said.

The scene that brought the house down was the three boys dancing to *YMCA*.

'If only Ryder and Jacinta were here,' Kent said.

'We can show them the video.'

'It'll probably go viral.' Kent chuckled.

Sophie and Kent were portrayed next, followed by Petie lying on the stage being attended to by characters representing Matt, the singer, and nurse, Bec Hunter, followed by Quinn and Kimberley, each scene being interspersed with the farting donkey, and Emily's words, 'Again, the power of love ensured that true love followed its course resulting in joy for this couple and the folk of

Augathella. It doesn't need to be Christmas to feel the joy in life.'

The curtain finally closed after a final appearance by the donkey, and a hungry cry from Ruby Rose. Thunderous applause and whistles filled the hall.

'More, more,' the crowd called. 'More donkey,' a boy's voice called from the front.

Emily took the microphone. 'We would like to invite all the cast to the stage to take a bow. Including the donkey.'

Braden leaned over to Callie. 'Do you realise what a high the three boys are going to be on tonight?'

'But how proud are you, Dad?' she asked.

'Absolutely bursting,' Braden said as the cast came onto the stage.

To their dismay and mirth, the donkey took centre stage as Rory and Nigel were revealed respectively as the front and rear end of the

163

donkey. Petie ran out and held up the whoopee cushion to much laughter.

'Well, it sure is a different take on the nativity play,' Braden said.

'But absolutely beautiful,' Callie said as they stood to make their way to the stage.

EPILOGUE

Callie

The catered supper was a huge success, and the crowd stayed until the food was gone, and Jenna began to pack up. Braden went down to collect the twins and brought Ruth back, and she'd already watched the video on Jon's camera, while nursing Ophelia.

As Callie stood watching Ruth laugh, a gentle hand touched her elbow.

'Callie?' She turned and smiled. Luke and Emily stood beside her. Luke's arm was around her shoulders, and Emily's face was alight with joy.

Callie shook her head. 'You are one amazing woman, Emily.'

'She is, isn't she?' Luke's smile was as wide as Emily's and Callie's heart filled with joy for them.

'It's certainly been a joyous night,' she said.

'Thank you. 'Emily's cheeks flushed pink as she looked up at Luke. Her eyes switched back to Callie. 'I wanted to thank you and Braden but he's busy stacking the chairs away, and we have to go now.'

'Thanks to your boys, Luke and I are going out to dinner to celebrate our engagement. If we don't hurry, the bistro will be closed.' Emily held out her hand. A single diamond on a gold band graced her ring finger.

'Oh, my goodness, that is such good news.' Callie hugged Emily and then Luke too. 'You have made my night, and what a night for it to happen!'

'Love and joy in Augathella,' Emily said. 'And we're engaged because of your boys.'

Callie frowned. 'How? What have they been up to?'

'It's a long story, Callie, but I've been carrying a lot of grief, and when I read their story last week, it made me realise what I had been missing all the time. Rory and Nigel showed me the power of love. I will be forever grateful to them.'

'And so will I.' Luke's arm went around Emily again and he pulled her close.

'Congratulations. Now, you two scoot, and I'll help Bob lock up.'

'One more thing. We'd like the three boys to be page boys at our wedding. We're getting married in January, so we can go away before term starts. Would you ask them?'

'With great pleasure.' Callie stood back and smiled widely as Luke and Emily headed out for their special dinner.

It looked like next year was going to begin with more love and joy in their town. Callie headed over to Braden, her heart bursting with love for her husband and their five beautiful children.

THE END

Who's getting married?

Pre-orders available for:

An Augathella Wedding

eBook:

https://www.amazon.com.au/Augathella-Christmas-Short-Sweet-Book-ebook/dp/B0CPYJC8CZ/

PRINT:

https://annieseatonstore.ecwid.com/

OTHER BOOKS FROM ANNIE

Daughters of the Darling
From Across the Sea
Over the River (2024)

Porter Sisters Series
Kakadu Sunset
Daintree
Diamond Sky
Hidden Valley
Larapinta
Kakadu Dawn

Pentecost Island Series
Pippa
Eliza
Nell
Tamsin
Evie
Cherry
Odessa
Sienna
Tess
Isla

The Augathella Girls Series
Outback Roads
Outback Sky
Outback Escape
Outback Wind

Annie Seaton

Outback Dawn
Outback Moonlight
Outback Dust
Outback Hope

An Augathella Surprise
An Augathella Baby
An Augathella Spring
An Augathella Christmas

Sunshine Coast Series
Waiting for Ana
The Trouble with Jack
Healing His Heart
Sunshine Coast Boxed Set

The Richards Brothers Series
The Trouble with Paradise
Marry in Haste
Outback Sunrise
Richards Brothers Boxed Set

Bondi Beach Love Series
Beach House
Beach Music
Beach Walk
Beach Dreams
The House on the Hill

Second Chance Bay Series
Her Outback Playboy
Her Outback Protector

An Augathella Christmas

Her Outback Haven
Her Outback Paradise
The McDougalls of Second Chance Bay Boxed Set

Love Across Time Series
Come Back to Me
Follow Me
Finding Home
The Threads that Bind
Love Across Time 1-4 Boxed Set

Bindarra Creek
Worth the Wait
Full Circle
Secrets of River Cottage
A Clever Christmas
A Place to Belong

Others
Whitsunday Dawn
Undara
Osprey Reef
East of Alice
Four Seasons Short and Sweet
Follow the Sun
Ten Days in Paradise
Deadly Secrets
Adventures in Time
Silver Valley Witch
The Emerald Necklace
A Clever Christmas

Annie Seaton

Christmas with the Boss
Her Christmas Star

ABOUT THE AUTHOR

Annie lives in Australia, on the beautiful north coast of New South Wales. She sits in her writing chair and looks out over the tranquil Pacific Ocean.

She writes contemporary romance and loves telling stories that always have a happily ever after. She lives with her very own hero of many years and they share their home with Toby, the naughtiest dog in the universe, and Barney, the ragdoll puss, who hides when the four grandchildren come to visit.

Stay up to date with her latest releases at her website: http://www.annieseaton.net

AWARDS

2023: Winner of the long contemporary RUBY award for Larapinta

Finalist for the NZ KORU Award 2018 and 2020.

Winner ...Best Established Author of the Year 2017 AUSROM

Longlisted for the Sisters in Crime Davitt Awards 2016, 2017, 2018, 2019

Finalist in Book of the Year, Long Romance, RWA Ruby Awards 2016 Kakadu Sunset

Winner ...Best Established Author of the Year 2015 AUSROM

Winner ...Author of the Year 2014 AUSROM
Best Established Author, Ausrom Readers' Choice 2017 Book of the Year

Milton Keynes UK
Ingram Content Group UK Ltd.
UKHW010847211223
434780UK00001B/24

9 781923 048225